To Tell You The Truth

To Tell You The Truth

∞

Enid Levinger Powell

Copyright © 2008 by Enid Levinger Powell.

Library of Congress Control Number: 2008906758
ISBN: Softcover 978-1-4363-5885-9

All rights reserved. No part of this book may be reproduced or transmitted in any form or by any means, electronic or mechanical, including photocopying, recording, or by any information storage and retrieval system, without permission in writing from the copyright owner.

This is a work of fiction. Names, characters, places and incidents either are the product of the author's imagination or are used fictitiously, and any resemblance to any actual persons, living or dead, events, or locales is entirely coincidental.

This book was printed in the United States of America.

To order additional copies of this book, contact:
Xlibris Corporation
1-888-795-4274
www.Xlibris.com
Orders@Xlibris.com

Contents

LEGACY

Bloodroot	23
Loving Aunt Gracie	29
Broken Spells	35
Following Directions	43
To Tell You the Truth	49
If You're Going to Cry	57
Leaving Home	65
Scenes with a View	71
'Til Death Do Us Part	77

FANTASIES AND FABRICATIONS

Borrowed Time	81
The Man Who Won Everything	85
Once Upon a Time	97
At the Heart of a Secret	101
The Real Thing	105
The Little Woman	115

THE HAND THAT YOU'RE DEALT

Homework	123
Radishes and Daffodils	129
Santa Claus Is a Man	135
Laugh Lines	143
If You Need Me	149
The Nature of the Game	155
Stockpiling	163

This book of stories is dedicated to my husband, Bert, whose unstinting support and enthusiasm never faltered; to my children, Pip Lowe and Jon Powell, who donated blocks of their childhood, "because Mom is writing"; to my grandchildren, Julian Lowe, and Natasha and Halle Powell, who made the publication of this book necessary; and to my parents, Selma and Herbert Levinger, my brother, Jeffrey Levinger, and my sister, Andrea Smith, who share my memories, albeit their versions may differ.

Preface

(For the Curious Reader)

Readers often believe that writers draw directly from their own lives . . . that we don't make anything up. Some critics have alleged that even what seems like an obviously imaginary story still comes from the writer's unconscious and therefore is, whether the writer owns up to it or not, autobiography.

The truth is (and we should be wary of anyone presuming to know, but still . . .) that few people are lucky enough to have memories that automatically turn into short stories or novels or plays. That all the writer has to do is write them down—or type them up. But Memory is a tricky muse. Many families, when discussing an incident from their shared past, have discovered that every person recalls it differently or has a different interpretation. Even a so-called memoir is, to be fair, just the author's point of view. That's one reason why I admire *The Liar's Club* in which the author admits that her sister would have a different view of the same experience. But the writer in the family gets to give her side.

So what is autobiographical fiction, a curious reader may ask?

After putting this collection of short stories together, and discovering that they run the gamut from stories with similar characters, to stories that were stimulated by an idea in a newspaper article, to stories whose source is a total mystery to me, I found one answer in the quilts my mother collected.

Think of a quilt made up of scraps saved from the quilter's life. A flannel shirt worn the first day of kindergarten; a piece of lace from a communion dress; a grandparent's favorite scarf. Each scrap calls up an emotion that accompanies the memory. The quilter chooses those scraps that connect emotional relevance to design possibilities. Eventually, the quilter/designer stitches a particular group of scraps together with the thread of imagination in order to create an artistic pattern. (Those scraps didn't simply fall into a heap when accidentally dropped on the floor.)

The writer also may choose among her life experiences (fabrics) those that seem to connect emotional relevance to story possibilities. Rarely, however, are these personal experiences sufficient. Therefore, she includes (from memory and journals) her observations of other people and even the stories they tell about their own lives. Finally, "what if" questions are tossed into the story (like a game made up of random words written on cubes or magnetic pieces) to see what turns up. What if the character is older, writes greeting cards, never owned a bicycle? Real life events may have been separated widely in time and space but the writer may decide to place them all in one location, at a specific time, if she discovers that the meaning of her design demands it.

The point is, none of these creations—quilts or stories—exist until a "designer" arranges the components in a form that pleases her. It is the hope for and joy of discovery that drives the creator to keep seeking connections . . . and creating new designs (meanings). The writer also hopes that her readers will find those hard-won discoveries equally meaningful.

Special Acknowledgments

My creative writing workshops have brought me not only the joy of teaching, but the joy of working with a group of writers who exemplify the value of trust when sharing work. As they have told me, and I them, we know things about each other, through our writing, that our families and other friends don't know and perhaps don't even suspect. That's because we write the truth as best we can figure it out. These truths should not be confused with facts. Facts are merely stitches in the fabric of our lives. We discover these truths as we try to incorporate the facts into an artistic piece of work. I say "we" because I have given my work to them for their critiques and feedback—it seemed only fair for them to have a shot at me.

I must first acknowledge the extraordinary support of four of my writers who have gone beyond what any normal person has a right to expect:

Carma Lynn Park, the Boswell to my Samuel Johnson (as she has termed our relationship) has typed and retyped every single story I wrote for this book, both published and unpublished. She has critiqued them as she went along, never holding back her opinions or limiting her hours. She also took on the role of organizing the materials for the publisher—including finding the illustration for the cover. Invaluable just doesn't do it.

Scottie Kersta-Wilson, my computer guru, who is in charge of placing our work on our site, *www.breakthruwriting.com*, photographing our members (and me), brainstorming ideas for this book or ways to improve our site, and who publishes the chapbooks of our members' work. Indispensable just doesn't do it.

Randall Van Vynckt, who volunteered to proofread and copyedit the manuscript before submission to the publisher, and happened to mention he is also a graphic artist, thereby having dumped on him the added role of designer for our front and back covers, with vital tweaks from Carma and Scottie until we thought we heard the covers scream stop! Indefatigable just doesn't do it.

Benjamin Polk, to whose eagle-eye and experienced editorship we entrusted the galleys for final proofreading and last-minute enhancements. Dedicated just doesn't do it.

Additional Acknowledgements

I must also acknowledge the students in my workshops now (and in the past) who inspired me to keep writing and learning, and whose feedback I find necessary—and generous. I will forever be grateful for their honest responses and terrific ideas. I'd like to take credit, as their teacher, but I know better.

This is a non-exhaustive list of the members of my workshops who have given me far more than I've given them: Annie Morgan, Alene Frost, Barbara Zoub, Deborah Holton, Deborah Hymanson, Denise Lanton, Diana Sebek, Eric Sutherlin, Erin Goseer Mitchell, Gloria Cecelia Valentino, John Moriarty, Kathy Mirkin, Kathy Simon, Kim de Somer, Leilani Garrett, Linda Fraden, Lois Roelofs, Mary Hutchings Reed, Meg Ciccantelli, Marilyn Knapp Litt, Myra Jesky, Nancy Freyburger, Noreen Kelly, Pam Spence, O.A. Marino, Peggy Brady Ross, Rion Klawinski, Sel Yackley, Sharon Durling, Sheila Peters, Sherry Holland, Shirley O'Rourke, Stephen Reidy, Sue Gray, Susan Tarrence and Wendy Grossman.

I could go on and on but even writers with a thesaurus can never find enough words when it comes to gratitude.

Formal Acknowledgements

Of course, I am forever obliged to the historic **Newberry Library** in Chicago, for including my writing workshop seminars on their roster of classes in the Arts & Humanities.

Finally, a warm thank you to the soap opera "The Young and the Restless" for employing me for ten years, for sharpening my dialogue, and for my pension, which allows me to keep writing.

Publishing Acknowledgments

Grateful acknowledgment is made to the editors of the following publications in which stories in this collection originally appeared, some in slightly different form:

CPU Review	"Homework"
Lilith	"Bloodroot"
McCall's	"Leaving Home"
Passages North	"Scenes with a View"
Syzygy 6	"The Little Woman"
The Mississippi Valley Review	"Radishes and Daffodils" and "The Real Thing"
The Husk	"Loving Aunt Gracie"
The Sign	"Broken Spells" and "Once Upon a Time"
Times-Outlook	"Santa Claus Is a Man"
True Love	"Borrowed Time"
Woman's World	"Laugh Lines"
Yankee	"Following Directions"

Legacy

Bloodroot

My grandmother loved one person in the world. Me. For me, always a smile, never a no. Even on the Sabbath she let me color in my coloring book. Me, alone, she tempted with jelly-filled doughnuts and other sweets my working mother deplored. "Eat, Ninotchka, eat," was her constant refrain. Then she'd sip her boiling tea while I would ask, with a mouth full of sugar, what was it like when she was a girl.

"The men were all afraid of me."

I chewed, content.

My grandfather boasted that my grandmother was the bravest, most exciting woman in their Russian village. After he escaped a Cossack sweep for Jewish men, she insisted he leave her behind with their two children and flee to America. After three years of painstaking tailoring, hunched in a dark shop, he sent for his family, who had found refuge in the dirt cellar of a sympathetic peasant. Much later I overheard my bachelor uncles whisper that she probably terrified the poor soul into silence.

"Why were the men afraid of you?" I asked, although I knew that everyone was afraid of her. Except me, of course. Tall for a woman, at five-foot-seven, she towered over my older uncle and her three daughters—my tiny mother and her older sister, Sally. Aunt Gracie, the youngest of the girls, and my younger uncle, Ari, though both taller than Grandma, always stooped beneath her cool scrutiny and seemed shorter. She was handsome, in that regal, fierce Mongolian style. Her black hair, tightly drawn back, sharpened her high cheekbones. The bony sockets of her eyes shadowed whatever color gleamed in those caverns.

"Why were the men afraid of you," I repeated. I liked to hear the answer.

"Fear or be feared." She would shrug, then bark her harsh laugh.

My uncles brought home their paychecks for her to deposit in accounts she kept for them. Uncle Murray, the eldest, languished in the bookkeeping job that Grandma considered suitable. He taught folk-dancing at night at the Y, despite Grandma's disapproval of such foolishness. As for Uncle Ari, her most compliant child, no one knew if his nervousness began when Grandma refused to let him play the piano because she didn't want to waste the violin given them by some debtor of my grandfather's. But when the other children sneaked Ari into their piano lessons, the teacher, recognizing Ari's gift, offered to give him free lessons. So Grandma relented. He eventually became a messenger, traveling around New York with a briefcase locked to his wrist.

One morning Uncle Murray tried to push another boundary.

"Acting?" My grandmother squared off immediately. "You think acting is something to do?"

Uncle Murray peeled an orange at the kitchen sink. "I'll have the lead—it's a radio play." He gestured toward the huge box nearly barring the way from the kitchen to the hall. My grandmother would sit open-mouthed before the webbed speaker during news broadcasts. My uncle said, "If there's an earthquake in Japan, she has to know if any Jews were killed." At night she riveted her shadowed eyes on my grandfather while he read the *Daily Forward* to her before dinner.

"A play," my grandmother mimicked my uncle. "A play is playing. So you want to play? So I'll buy you a toy." She barked her laugh.

"The rehearsals are only at night," my uncle said, digging harder into the peel.

"So Borden needs a bookkeeper falling asleep?"

"I'll be home late," he said, and dropped the half-peeled orange into the garbage in his rush to the door.

"Throw away good food?" my grandmother shrieked after him. "Starve to death—then see how long you play."

I flew after my uncle, catching him half way through the door. He bent and squeezed a kiss against my forehead before stomping down the street.

The family rarely ate together except at the High Holidays. A terrible cook, Grandma put a chicken in a pot of boiling water on the back of the stove and kept it warm there until one or another family member claimed a piece of bleached meat and bowl of soup—usually after Grandma stalked to the stove to loudly inquire who had not yet eaten and did they think they could stay alive without a good hot meal.

I crept back to my grandmother, who was singing to herself in the kitchen. Hearing me, she said, "Ninotchka—come—Grandma will peel you a nice orange."

"No," I said, trembling.

"An egg—a boiled egg and piece of toast. Come."

"No."

She wiped her hands down the front of her apron. "Okay, okay, but when you're hungry don't come to me." The eyes glistened like water in an underground pool. She grumbled about all our bony bodies, but no one was thinner than she.

I thrust my chin out, daring her.

"Come, Ninotchka," she said softly, melting the lines in her face into their special arrangement for me. "Come, we'll walk by Mr. Petchal's. I bet he has a chocolate doughnut."

"No." But I shifted my feet, inclining one hip towards her.

"And the ten cents store—paper dolls with new dresses to cut."

I hung my head.

"Ninotchka," a whisper. "Murray ain't mad. You'll see. When he comes home, he'll play hiding with you. Come."

"A coloring book?" I whispered back.

She took my willing hand. "Come, Ninotchka. Your grandma will make you happy. And later we'll hear the radio. Listen to your grandma."

Uncle Murray put in twenty-five years as a bookkeeper, but he did turn down all the young women my grandmother suggested he marry. "A bachelor is a disgrace," she would harangue, but he lived at home until she died.

Only my father, whom my widowed mother married when I was five, worked out a lighthearted relationship with my grandmother. She permitted him to tease her about my mother's imprecise birth date, tied, as was the custom, to the nearest religious holiday. "How come," Dad once asked, "Lily was born six months after you arrived in this country?"

Grandma shrugged. "Maybe the date I came here, I got it wrong."

"Maybe some blond Cossack . . . ?"

Her eyes glittering, Grandma merely barked with laughter.

My grandmother called me "The Little Shiksa," in a tone oddly soft. She never called my mother that, although we both had blond hair and green eyes. When Grandma paraded me down the dense Brooklyn streets, her neighbors would pat my hair and marvel, "She doesn't look Jewish, does she? A regular Shirley Temple." My grandmother would nod coldly, and, taking my cue, I dipped my head modestly.

Grandma and I had one regular outing on the streetcar to visit her sister-in-law whom she despised. My grandfather's sister was as plump as the cushions stuffed about her brocaded apartment. She had no children and cuddled me unmercifully under my grandmother's icy stare.

"Such a skinny one she is," my great-aunt would say.

Grandma's eyes gleamed but she only shrugged. "She eats."

"If I had her with me, she'd show some flesh," the woman continued.

"If I ever want her stuffed, I'll think on it," Grandma responded. "But I've heard too much flesh can make a woman barren. Not that I'm such an expert."

I could see the heavy roll on the woman's neck redden, and the next remarks would fly in Yiddish. Nevertheless, the aunt always sent us home laden with packages of expensive children's clothing that my mother would smooth gently and shake her head at.

Grandma, however, pressed her bony fingers against the pounding in her skull and cursed her sister-in-law's selfishness.

"Why do you put yourself through it?" my mother asked. "Are these coats and dresses worth your aggravation?"

Grandma paused in her head massage to level a finger at my mother. "Would she send one rag of underwear? No. I should first go to her fine home, walk on her carpets—eat off her dishes—then she gives."

"But it makes you ill."

The contemptuous smile fought with the pain on my grandmother's face. "And after she sees Ninotchka, her Harry tells your father she is sick for days. They thought gold could make babies. Now they rot alone in their fancy apartment."

"So you'll kill yourself for a bit of silk and velvet?"

Grandma rose to her full height, towering over both of us. "They owe Nina. Who else do they have? But with some—" and her eyes seemed to sink deeper, as if into memory—"with some you have to let them see a little . . . suffering . . . before they'll save even a child." She raised her fist. "So I make sure I give them back pain for pain."

"That's revenge—sickness," my mother whispered.

But my grandmother heard and we both trembled at the menace with which she said, "You know nothing—nothing about revenge. Revenge," she concluded, "is justice."

She eventually made that clear to me. On one of our returns from the great-aunt, we were more loaded down than ever, struggling to thrust ourselves and our packages through the trolley door and down the steep steps. Apparently in a rush, the driver didn't allow time for us both to alight, catching my coat in the closing doors. My cry of fear was lost in my grandmother's screeching. When the driver, alerted by frantic passengers, finally reopened the doors, my grandmother crushed me against her and began to curse the man in high-decibel Yiddish sprinkled with some English "dog" and "Cossack." The driver, taking tone for content, shook his fist and shouted, "Shut up, you dirty Jew!"

As he drove off, Grandma dropped me to her side. Her eyes seemed to disappear into their craters. Her fists doubled and her throat bulged with sound. She ran alongside the trolley, yelling, spittle flying in the air while I screamed as she dashed away from me. Quickly outdistanced by the trolley, she stood gasping in the street until I ran up to lean against her. Her hair had loosened, and wisps of black streamed witch-like around her face.

"He'll go to jail," she vowed, bending over me. "He can't say that—not to me." I trembled against her, in a kind of exalted terror.

According to family lore, Grandma did indeed bring the man to court. Among my grandfather's customers she found and bullied a lawyer into taking the case. With time and location documented, they found the driver. How clearly I can envision my grandmother, eyes hooded, informing the judge, in a quieter though equally vehement tone, that in America no man could call her a dirty Jew. To everyone's surprise the judge agreed and fined the driver, who paid a small sum in red-faced disbelief.

When my grandmother died in her seventies, my uncles bragged she had not one gray hair, nor had she shrunk one inch. She had, however, saved the paychecks she'd demanded they turn over to her, and left each of them a substantial account.

After being told for years that I was just like my grandmother (unaware that it was not entirely a compliment), I began, when I entered college, to search for traces of her in myself. I dated happily until a golden basketball player focused his Teutonic attention on me. Immediately, my status rose with my sorority pledge sisters . . . and myself. I masked my anxiety to please with attempts at humorous self-deprecation. He introduced me to his friends as a "brain," grinning to show how illogical it was to find one housed in me. Recognizing my cue, I laughed, too.

"You know," he finally said, after an evening in which we emptied ourselves of every detail of our past, "you don't look Jewish."

An automatic smile, twin to his, began forming on my lips. Then died. I felt as if my eyes were disappearing into caverns. I barked a contemptuous laugh.

"I don't consider that a compliment," I said coldly.

He froze, in what looked to me like fear. I felt brave and exciting.

Eventually, I married a dark, neat man, and our daughter is as small-boned as he. My son, however, is very tall and fair, with enormous hands and feet and blue Cossack eyes.

Loving Aunt Gracie

Until my ninth summer I loved Aunt Gracie uncritically, passionately, from the tip of her high-piled orange hair down to the rhinestone bracelet encircling her slim ankle. I would have been even more impressed had I known that the stunning color was the result of brown hair bleached blond, then hennaed until it seemed her whole head was gloriously on fire. Her eyes, with the black lashes she carefully pasted on, and the royal blue painted lovingly over each lid, thrilled me more than any movie star's. Aunt Gracie also drew beautiful wine-red circles on her cheeks and outlined her eyebrows with a thick black pencil. I believed that my extraordinary aunt was one of a chosen few born without fuzzy eyebrow hairs, and I thought everyone else looked colorless and sickly in comparison.

When we'd go for a walk for a chocolate soda, or a Coke, or a new lipstick, I would skip beside her, proudly conscious of heads swiveling in our direction, of stifled gasps of admiration and mouths falling open in envy. It was delicious knowing my aunt was the most beautiful, the most kind, the most talented woman in the whole world. I would add a silent parenthesis of apology, "Except for my mother, of course." My mother was wonderful, too, in her soft way, but she had to work during the day, and Aunt Gracie worked at night. My mother said she was a dancer on Broadway and although I begged to be allowed to see her perform, my pleas fell on reddened ears.

"Perform," my grandmother snorted. "Parade's more like it."

"Not my niece." One of my bachelor uncles would pound on the table.

"But it's all so pretty, so shiny," Aunt Gracie would say in a bewildered tone. She loved her "career."

"It's like a fairyland, honey," she often said to me. "And we wear the most beautiful things. Long, silk skirts, and great big hats with flowers, and lights all shining on us, and music soaring all around. The loveliest thing in the world. And I have six different costumes every show. Six of them! One time I had eight, and one of them was a little bitty thing with sequins." Her eyes would glow even bluer as she spoke, and she'd smooth her dress, or pat a curl in place, and I would ache to see it all—to touch the silky dresses and rub my cheek in the furry trims, as Aunt Gracie said she did.

But all I ever got for my tears and pleadings were a shush from my mother and a bedtime story from Aunt Gracie before she had to leave. I loved to watch her long, crayon-red fingernails turn the pages. The rest of her hands, arms and legs was pure white, and she wore dazzling dresses of purple and bright green, and red and black, which she assured me were very much like her costumes in the show. Her bracelets and necklaces jingled and jangled until, overcome with ecstasy, I would throw myself on her, squeezing the soft body and gasping in the wonderful scents of perfume, powder and magical creamy things I longed to know about.

"Oh, Aunt Gracie, will I be like you?" I asked.

"You'll be much, much better," she whispered back.

"Will I ever be as pretty?"

"Much, much prettier."

"Will I smell as good?"

"Much, much sweeter."

"How do you know?"

"Because I love you," she always said.

That day at the beach began just like our other jaunts. As usual, Aunt Gracie broke a date when I expressed my desire to go the first warm Saturday. I hardly needed more than a tear or two, and maybe one dry sob, before she was on the phone to Mike, or Joe, or Leonard. Sometimes one of them went with us, which I disliked except for the presents her beaus always brought me. The same man rarely offered to accompany us twice. I could hear Howard, this time, yell over the phone, and I could see Aunt Gracie's lip tremble. Her lip always trembled whenever someone raised his voice to her, which I had guessed was what the family meant when they'd whisper, thinking me asleep, that she was just like a child.

I'd hear my uncle grumble, "It's impossible anyone could be so guileless, so naïve—anyone except my sister!"

My mother would answer in her soothing way, "Gracie was always like this. And always will be. She thinks she's surrounded by glamour at that place. She's a baby—a big, beautiful, bouncy baby. She and Nina adore each other. They speak the same language."

I was confused, particularly about Aunt Gracie and I both speaking English, but watching her on the phone, I had to admit she did sound like a baby.

"How can you be so cruel," Aunt Gracie's voice quavered. "The poor, fatherless child, just a tiny baby, and she wants only a few hours of fun." Then her voice got angrier, and she finally stamped her high-heeled foot, as I was not allowed to do, and cried, "Well, I'm very glad to know how you feel and believe me, I'd never dream of going out with a man who hates helpless little children."

She slammed down the receiver, then gave me a hug, telling me we were going, and my private sun shone warm and safe as ever.

We always wore our bathing suits under our clothing to save time so we could go directly to the beach and find a good spot, instead of first undressing in the wooden stalls. We chose a clear circle of sand for our blankets, and my pail and shovel and beach ball, and Aunt Gracie's satchel that held tantalizing bottles with thick and thin creams, and little packets of eyelashes, and big and little brushes for hair, eyebrows, and colors for her skin. We sat very far back from the ocean. Once, Aunt Gracie had stood near the water's edge, and when she felt the sand shift beneath her feet, she had screamed the tide was carrying her out and fainted. Luckily the family was there and calmed her when she woke up and screamed to get away from the water. I wasn't afraid of the water, but I never went near it when I was alone with my aunt. I understood what it was like to be afraid of things like the dark and what was under the bed.

I pulled off my sunsuit and waited for Aunt Gracie to slip out of her skirt and blouse so I could bury her under pails full of sand. When her skirt fell to her ankles, an unfamiliar feeling froze me to the point of pain. All I could see were acres and acres of pure white skin. She mistook my open-mouthed horror for admiration and patted her bare stomach.

"How do you like it?" She smiled. "I wear it in a bathing scene at the theater, and I knew it would be perfect here, too. Now I can get a really good tan. Come—hand Aunt Gracie that bottle in there."

I was rooted to each grain of hot sand beneath me. I felt as if I was simultaneously falling and doomed to stand there forever. Over Aunt Gracie's shoulder I could see other women in two-piece suits, but the pieces were much larger than Aunt Gracie's. Then I saw their faces and the faces of the men nearby. I heard the stifled gasps and saw strange smiles. I felt heads turning on either side of me, but my own neck was rigid.

"Darling, what's wrong? You're white. Here, sit next to me." She patted the space on the blanket, leaning forward. Her top was not like the tops of the other women. I started to shake.

"I'm going to throw up," I said.

Aunt Gracie didn't waste time gathering our things together. She rushed me home as if our lives were in danger, which was her reaction to any illness. I refused her fluttering hands and didn't say another word until we reached home. My mother was there, and I ran into her arms. I cried and sobbed and raged, but I wouldn't talk. When she asked me what happened, I could only shake my head. Finally she put me to bed.

"Don't let Aunt Gracie in," I whispered. I felt my face burn and turned to the wall. I thought I would be sick all over again.

My mother remained calm. "All right," she said, "You can see her in the morning."

"No!" I shouted. Then muffling it into my pillow, "No." I cried myself to sleep.

Aunt Gracie stayed home from her beloved job that night. No one could convince her that I was all right. She kept a vigil outside my door, sitting with the chair sideways so that when I padded out of my room in the morning, I fell into her lap. She gathered me into her arms and started smoothing my hair, murmuring softly. I tore away and ran into the bathroom, locking the door. When I heard her run to my mother, screaming, "The baby is sick again. Call the doctor!" I ran back into my room.

My mother made me get dressed. She only said, "You can't stay in your room forever. You're a big girl now." She looked as if she wanted to say more, her eyes searching my face for help, but she evidently found none.

I refused to accompany Aunt Gracie to the store after breakfast, but I watched her through the window. Soon I saw her returning. Her hips undulating, her bracelets jangling harshly in the soft, morning air, her glaring hair seemingly piled even higher because she always held her head so straight, as if a basket of fruit was balanced precariously there. I could see neighbors turn to stare at the spiky eyelashes, the brilliant blue eyelids, the strange purplish cheeks. Near our house she glanced up and saw me. Her lips widened, and she walked to the window holding up a dripping paper bag.

Her generously lipsticked mouth framed the words, "Ice cream." She raised her inverted-V eyebrows. "Want some?"

I turned slightly but watched her from the corner of my eye. I saw her hand press her throat as she waited, looking up at me. Her eyes had shadows beneath, and I saw her lower lip tremble and then catch between her teeth. A little ice cream trickled down from the bag she was still holding aloft. A puff of wind blew her skirt and drew my attention to the rhinestone ankle bracelet. I looked quickly back to her face. She blinked rapidly and started to lower her arm, her bright head drooping on her neck. A sob escaped me, and suddenly I ran down the stairs, out the door and into her arms.

"I love you," I cried. "Believe me, Aunt Gracie, I do love you."

She hugged me to her. "I know, darling," she said, patting my head. "I know you do." But I couldn't stop crying.

Broken Spells

I turned five the month after my widowed mother married Karl Levin. We went to live in a bungalow hidden behind my new grandfather's house. As in fairy tales, a father had suddenly appeared as miraculously and undeservedly as the unknown one had disappeared; a dream home, with my very own room—even a ruffled dressing table—bloomed into reality.

True, the bungalow, one block from the ocean, was rented out in the summer and we three moved into the big house where the new grandfather I hated ruled us all. But this seasonal repossession by "others" fitted my explanation of existence. I knew that bad witches cast spells that lasted only until good fairies outwitted them. Life was just a matter of waiting out the bad spells with their inexplicable rules: magic circles one couldn't cross; foods not to be tasted; doors not to be opened.

I was not a questioning child. I had too many questions, I think, and since I couldn't frame the first, could not, therefore, go on to the next. So I accepted my grandfather's rules, too. No bathing suits worn on the front porch, not even to cross inside; no food left over on plates; no child may touch the piano.

I broke the piano rule the first Sunday we visited the big house. I had been excused from the dinner table and wandered into the parlor from the hall door. My mother's brother had given me piano lessons the previous year, when I was four. I was picking out a tune, by trial and error, when suddenly the double doors to the dining room crashed open and my short, barrel-chested grandfather strode to the piano and slammed the lid.

"There will be no children practicing in this house," he roared.

Before I could scramble from the piano bench, my new father scooped me up. "Hey," he said, "it's all right, Nina. You didn't know."

I put my head into his shoulder and allowed the comfort to continue. As my father carried me out he explained, "Grandpa's back is hurt and he has pain all the time. People in pain can't listen to little children practice—especially people who know a lot about music."

I lifted my head. "Does he play the piano, too?"

My father rubbed his chin in my hair. "No. But I'll show you what he used to do." He took me to my grandfather's room. "Those are famous opera singers," he said, pointing to framed and signed photographs. My grandfather had been an assistant manager for the Metropolitan Opera before his car accident. He still broke into Wagnerian themes regularly, his thick gray hair, once red as rust, springing to life as he sang and tossed his head.

I studied the pictures and noticed that my grandfather was in some of them, shaking hands or with an arm flung over his shoulder.

"Do they visit him?" I asked, ready to be touched by the famous.

"No," my father said quietly . . . then added, "He doesn't ask them to. He doesn't want—anyway, they don't." He whisked me out of the room as if we were escaping. Ghosts, I decided.

I never broke another rule. Coming home from the beach I had to enter the dark, spider-filled basement, undress in the chill damp, and appear for lunch in a freshly starched sunsuit, silent with hatred for this grandfather.

Yet I never asked to return to our previous home, the only one I had known. I never knew my real father. I was just two when he died and my mother had to return to work. We lived with her mother, brothers and sister where I ate nothing unless I was begged. They sighed to the ceiling but considered me too fair and delicate to deny. But later, when asked if I missed Grandma Rae, or Uncle Murray, I would shake my head because now I had a father, and even in the big house the three of us had our Sunday morning wrestling bout in the big bed while my mother laughed like a little girl.

My Grandma Rae and nervous uncles had kept me safely indoors unless one of them could personally take me somewhere. Therefore, when we moved I was terrified of bigger children, swings, seesaws and bicycles.

But this new grandfather didn't believe in the pain of skinned knees or snowballs thrown by boys from the nearby parochial school. "You go back out there and let them see you're not afraid," he shouted, sending me out like a manager does his fighter. Every held-back tear seemed to swell a bitter pool inside me that swore revenge.

The day before my sixth birthday, my mother gone for the day, my grandfather presented me with a tricycle. "Let me see you ride it," he said as I backed away.

"I can't."

"Of course you can," he growled and pointed to the seat.

I eased myself onto the small triangle of leather, the tips of my toes brushing the ground. "It's too big," I whispered.

"Put your feet on the pedals," he said.

I hauled each foot up separately, swaying, clutching the handlebars with slippery palms.

"Push down," he shouted. "Push the pedals down one at a time. Hurry up."

I knew I was going to fall and the pile of metal and rubber would land on me and I would bleed and cry and nothing could prevent it. I pushed on the pedals, first both of them, and then, accidentally, one of them. As that foot went down the other rose up, and the surprise pitched me over.

"Get up, get up," I heard him shouting through the cotton of my head. "You've got it. Do it again."

Sobbing, I found myself back on the seat, my feet hitched to the pedals. By the time my parents came home, I was speeding up and down the sidewalk. But when they bent to express their surprised pride, I showed them my skinned knee and wrinkled my mother's skirt with my tears.

In my eighth year we moved into the big house permanently. I didn't know that my father was recovering from a near-fatal illness, nor that the Depression was grinding on. To my unquestioning mind the inexplicable was still the rule: no more bungalow; mother away at some part-time job; grandfather my only greeter when I returned from school.

A daily ritual ensued. Timidly, I ascended the front porch steps, closed the front door, not letting the screen door slam, and asked if Jack Armstrong had started. Without a smile he would switch on the big radio and we would sit rapt before it for two hours while Tom Mix, the Lone Ranger and Captain Midnight worked their suspense on us.

Although he helped me send away for code rings, badges and periscopes, my grandfather's rule was inflexible. "That's another box of Ralston," he would warn me. For whatever boxtops we sent in, I had to eat the cereal inside. Ralston, Wheaties, Cream of Wheat.

"I'll eat it," I'd promise.

The next morning breakfast would be one sticky mass that refused to pass the constricted muscles of my throat without a glower from his pain-ridden eyes. My code ring burned on my finger.

On the rare occasions when I had to miss an episode, he listened alone and told me in gruff detail what my heroes had suffered and were being threatened by. While he listened he fashioned strange figures for me from lobster claws, lumpy potatoes, bits of cellophane and colored string.

I wanted to tell my mother, "I hate him—I hate him," but my father would be there, reaching for me. "Let's make a sandwich," he'd shout, and I would be hugged between him and my mother, the words buried one more time.

Often, when evening came and I had nothing to do, I would eventually approach my grandfather and ask, "Do you want to play checkers?"

"No."

"How about War?"

"No."

"A hand of rummy?"

"No."

Then, when he seemed about to either bury himself in his stamp collection or retreat to his room, I would blurt out desperately, "Casino?"

After a groan he would always say, "All right. But where are the cards?"

And I would whip them out from behind my back.

It never occurred to me to ask anyone else to play. My grandfather taught me the games, and just as elves had special gifts, I assumed these were his. Years afterwards I would hear one of my parents suddenly say, "Casino?" in a desperate tone, and the other would laugh and give in.

I never heard either parent remonstrate with my grandfather until his daughter came to visit from Oklahoma with her two boys. His only grandsons filled the house with noise and knobby knees, and I adored them as much for their superior years as for their abandon.

They talked pig-Latin in front of me until my tears moved the elder to translate. They bought dried apricots with our candy money. They slammed doors, obeying only the bathing-suit rule. They even invaded the parlor and played a duet on the piano one dusty afternoon before they waved good-bye and left me with a wistful affection that persisted over the years.

That evening I heard my father say, behind a half-open parlor door, "That's not fair, Pop. You can't let them play the piano and forbid Nina."

"Once and they're gone," my grandfather answered. "I can't put up with the clatter of a child practicing."

"But she can't understand that," my father insisted.

"Nina's an obedient child, not like those demons," my grandfather said. "She understands rules. She'll live among the elite some day, and they recognize quality."

Hearing them move toward the door, I fled to the bedroom I had to share with my parents in the big house. I crawled under my bed and lay on my stomach. In fairy tales magical people like my cousins are not bound by rules that bind others. Yet my father did say it wasn't fair. Before, I had accepted my grandfather as mean and wicked—that was his nature. Now resentment boiled in me.

I recalled how I had to force down bits of food to clean my plate, while he vowed that some day I would eat at the Waldorf-Astoria. In preparation, I had to break off a small piece of bread to push the food onto a spoon or fork. "You'll stay at the finest hotels," he would chant, after correcting my posture. I had never questioned the strange justice in fairy tales. But father Karl had *said* it wasn't fair.

What was the spell that kept the three of us bound? Was it that voice booming out of his room with strange words? My mother said he spoke seven languages. I knew that seven was a magical number.

I rolled out from under the bed and tiptoed to his bedroom door, which was slightly ajar. I pushed it and peeked into the room. The framed pictures stood on a dresser, with a few hung on the wall.

I stepped inside and took one of the photographs in my hands. A lady with her throat hidden by chins smiled back at me. She wore a fancy dress dipping off her shoulders. I tried to read the name scrawled across the bottom. I made out "love" and "Helen." She had the look of the rich and powerful queens in my stories. Next to her my grandfather held himself stiffly, not an inch over five feet, his chin parallel to his round chest. I tried to imagine that thick hair bright red, with red tufts above his brown eyes. But he was the color and texture of iron to me. And even when I heard him cursing in his room, or bursting into song, the sounds were gray filings in my mind.

If I broke the glass would I break the spell? I held the metal frame against my mouth. Suddenly, I let it drop. My ears rang from the tight breath in my throat, waiting for the crack. But the picture missed the wood floor and bounced harmlessly on the soft rug next to the bed. With numb fingers I replaced the photograph on the dresser.

My brother was born right before we moved to Chicago because of my father's new job. Magic again. A baby out of nowhere (my mother said I never asked the usual questions). Ahead, a train ride and a new home. But the rules first required my mother to stay away for four nights. On the last night I left my father a note that I suspected my grandfather would see. "I hate Grandpa," I wrote. "I always have and I always will. I don't care if he hurts."

That day June Locke had taken my best crayons and told the teacher they were hers. I rushed home knowing my grandfather was a friend of her parents. "Will you tell them?" I asked.

"You don't want to be a tattle-tale," he said.

I could hardly whisper the words, "But they're mine."

"Then *you* get them back," he said. "You don't get other people to fight your battles. You march over there and tell June to give you back those crayons or else."

I backed out of the dining room, ran down the porch steps and around to the back. Or else—what? June was stubborn. She never minded the spankings she got for lying. She wasn't afraid of anybody, although I believed she would be afraid of my grandfather. I picked up a heavy branch in the backyard and beat it against the ground. If only I could see it land on June's head, see the blood spurt, have her beg me to stop. "Not fair, not fair," I chanted.

I kept beating the earth as I walked to the front of the house and crossed the street. June was smirking on her porch, one hand on the screen door, ready to dash inside. I paused at the bottom step and pitched my voice to reach her, but not carry indoors where her mother might be. I squeezed the stick, scratching the bark against my palm, and tried to put menace into my stare.

"I'll tell my grandfather," I said through clenched teeth. "If you don't give back my crayons, I'll tell him and he'll come over—*right now*."

She glanced across the street and said suddenly, "Stay there. I don't want your old crayons. I was only teasing."

Her scabby legs disappeared into the house, and I wondered if I'd been tricked, but she just as quickly reappeared and threw the box down at me so that a few crayons rolled into the street.

"Stupid dope," I half-shouted, still afraid of attracting an adult, but as I gathered my crayons I felt an embarrassed triumph.

I rushed to my bedroom and hid the crayons in my drawer, yet I still felt wronged—by my grandfather, by June, by myself. I wanted to throw the crayons in his face. I rubbed my palm where the branch had made it sore and then decided to write that note.

I didn't cry when my grandfather died, only one month after we moved away, but I was uneasy overhearing my mother sigh that she thought it was because I wasn't there anymore. "Gave him something to get up in the morning for," she said.

In less than a year we were able to buy a piano and I began the first of seven years of lessons. My joy became another nodule of resentment to use retroactively against my grandfather. A talent almost blighted—as perfect in plot as any fairy tale.

Seven years later my cousins and I found ourselves reminiscing during their visit to celebrate my high school graduation and piano recital. I reminded them of their pig Latin and my incarceration in that awful house.

"You'll never know how it was," I said for the benefit of my little brother, who had never known his grandfather. "My mother said she tried to intervene, but we were living in *his house*. He made a big thing out of accepting a widow and her daughter for his only son. (I didn't know what I meant by that, but had once overheard my mother telling someone how unusual that was for such a proud man.)

"That was really a shame," the older cousin said, "especially when you consider he wasn't really your grandfather."

"How can you say that?" I blurted. "He w-was as much my—he certainly loved . . ."

I didn't dare finish in the glare of their surprise. I felt as if past images were composing before my eyes, like shifting pieces of colored glass in those kaleidoscopes my father gave me. As each piece slipped, a whole new design appeared. I wanted to stop the radio, the bicycle, the cards, the stiff, framed photographs.

I crossed my arms over the pressure in my chest. By acts of will—and love—he had transcended the barrier of blood. Now I, willing heir to those acts, transcended the barrier of time and gave myself my grandfather. The spell was finally broken.

Following Directions

I eye the curlers and thin tissue papers suspiciously as my mother pours a pink, pungent solution into a bowl. "Are you sure you won't get it too tight?" I ask. "The last one was too curly."

"This is a body wave," she says, holding up the box that blares "Body Wave" in aqua.

"I don't really care—but you're supposed to do a test curl first."

"We can test one of the curls after they're all on," she answers, smiling. "We can always take them out. Anyway, the test curl is for people with allergies."

"But it says on the directions." I hold out the tiny folder to her. It looks as if it has never been unfolded.

She shakes her head. "I glanced at them in the drug store. Never read all the directions at once. It gets too confusing. You read only one step and then do that step. Just like in sewing. So first thing you do is wash your hair."

"I washed it an hour ago. Nothing is going to help."

"Well, I had to get the roast started in case this takes longer than we expect."

"The *directions* say it takes twenty minutes."

She eases me to a kitchen chair. "That depends on your hair. And how long it takes to roll it up. Those end papers are little devils."

I sit down, obedient as ever. I want to believe. She makes my clothes, even pantsuits—and most of them turn out. I spread the direction folder out on the table.

"Not that it makes any difference," I say. I wince as she presses the rattail of the comb against my scalp, swallowing back tears that are too close.

"Sorry," she mumbles, and I know she has filled her mouth with curlers. I bet *that's* not in the directions.

"Let me hand you those, with the papers," I say. "It gives me something to do."

She drops the curlers and end papers in my lap. "That's a big help," she says, patting my shoulder. She is invariably grateful for any kind of favor.

I begin again. "It's a lot of work for nothing."

"It's going to come out perfectly lovely. You'll see."

"But what for? I mean who cares?"

"You said the spring dance is in two weeks."

"Three. But I'm not going."

"How do you know? Curler, please." She sounds crisply professional.

"Did you wet it too much?" I can feel a drop sliding down my forehead.

"You can't wet it too much. This just relaxes the hair."

"I need a towel. It's not supposed to get in your eyes."

She rummages in a kitchen drawer, then drops a small dish towel in my lap. "Use that and stop worrying."

"Why should I worry? If it's too tight, it's too tight. It loosens up eventually. Like in a year."

"Now listen." She pauses, then picks up the folder.

"What does it say?" I ask.

She tosses it back on the table and continues parting a back section of my hair. "Now where was I?"

I hold up a curler and sheet of end paper.

"Okay. You'll go to the dance, and your hair will look lovely."

"I'll only be going if Beverly fixes me up, and last time she must have dug the guy out of a coffin."

"Blind dates aren't all bad. You get to meet other people . . ."

"I will not go on a blind date again!" I say through my teeth.

"Well, maybe that boy you mentioned will ask you. Didn't he call here last week?"

"His name is Jerry. And he called yesterday—about the homework. So if he was going to ask me, he would've."

"Maybe he got cold feet and plans to call back."

"You don't know that. Why do you say things like you're sure when you don't know?" I blink hard and press the towel over my eyes.

"Did I drip some?" she asks, peering at me.

"Just a bit."

"Well, don't worry. The sides are next. They go fast."

"What did you do? Read the directions?"

She laughs.

"I don't see why we had to move anyway," I say. "Nobody moves their third year in high school."

"Your father had to accept this offer," she answers. "And you've already made some nice friends."

"By the time I get to know them we'll all be in colleges a thousand miles apart."

"You'll visit each other and get together on holidays."

"Wherever I go I'll have to start all over again. I shouldn't have skipped a grade."

"With your grades you can go wherever you want to."

"That's what I mean. I don't know where I want to go." I tear an end paper in pieces.

"Look at that. We're ready for the other side—then the front—and all done."

I hold up the folder. "Shouldn't you test a curl now?"

"The back is the toughest part and takes the longest."

"Will you run out of setting lotion?"

"Oh, no. They give you plenty. It's the neutralizer that counts—makes it permanent." She laughs.

"All they talk about is colleges and sororities. I'll never go into a sorority. They're all snobs."

"Some are very nice and you make good friends then, for your whole life."

"How do you know? You didn't go to college. You always talk as if you know things." The words make my stomach ache. I know she left high school to go to work. That's why she reads a lot, she says. She is great on reading everything but directions.

"I know lots of people who went to college and they loved it."

"Oh, sure. Best time of their lives." I shake my head.

"Keep your head still," she says. "I'm almost finished."

"I think you should test a curl."

"If it makes you feel better." I hear her unhook the elastic around one of the curlers.

"How does it look?"

"Perfect," she says.

"Like the picture?"

"Just like the picture. Exactly. As soon as I get the front up, we can rinse the back."

"Shouldn't you do it now?"

"No. It'll be just right after I get the front up."

"What if the phone rings?"
"Tell whoever it is to call back."
"No one is going to call anyway."
"I could make you one of those halter-top dresses you like." She starts humming "Two Little Girls in Blue."
"Now we rinse the back," she says. "Pull the chair over to the sink."
"I can't bend back that way."
"Just lean on your elbows," she says. "I'll pour the water through with a pitcher."

The water is cold against my neck and I cringe, pushing my shoulders up.

"Don't scrunch," she says. "I can't reach the little bottom curlers then."

I put my shoulders back and squeeze my hands into fists. "Aren't you supposed to use warm water?"

"This is warm. It just feels cold to you. Okay. Sit up."

When I do, she says, "Now I'll test the left side."

She sighs and I ask, "Well? How is it?"

"Just a little longer, I think. I better look at my roast while I have a chance."

Dabbing at my wet neck and back, I shiver as drops of water slide down inside my blouse.

"Oh, no," I hear her moan, and I whirl around.

"What is it? Did you lose the neutralizer?"

"No. Of course not. I just put the oven on too high. I'd better take the meat out now, and put it in again just before dinner. Your father likes it rare."

"Shouldn't you test a curl again?"

"In just a minute."

"Take your time," I say. "If it's too curly, it's too curly. I don't care anymore."

"It will be perfectly lovely," she says. "Would you like a little taste of roast?"

I turn away. "No, thank you."

I feel her at my head again. "There. Just right. Rinse time."

I bend over sideways, and she pours water over my temples. "That'll do it," she says, as I rise, unable to bend in that position any longer. "Now one more side and . . ."

The phone rings and I stare, blinking water out of my eyes.

"I'll get it," she says. "Whoever it is can call back."

"No!" I shout. "Let me get it."

I rush into the hall and pick up the receiver in the middle of the third ring. "How are you doing?" asks my father.

"Awful."

I hand the phone to my mother.

"Hi. Will you be home on time?" A pause. "Oh, dear," she says, sounding disappointed. "I already put the roast in and I'm afraid it'll be a bit overdone by the time you get here." Another pause, then, "That's a good idea. I'll leave it out for awhile and see if that helps."

When she returns, I ask, "Isn't that sneaky?"

"Your father likes to feel he's helping me."

She busies her fingers at my head, then, "I think we can rinse now. Oh, I just can't wait to see how beautiful it's going to be. You have the loveliest hair and it takes a curl so well."

The rinsing done, she pours a powder into another bowl. "Where's the measuring cup?" she asks. "We need to add one-quarter cup of water. Or is it one-half?"

I hand her the directions without speaking.

"One-third," she reads. "Where *is* my measuring cup?"

We poke through the cupboards and drawers, and I feel my jaw and throat tighten, but I will not speak.

Suddenly she whoops, "Found it! And isn't it lucky it's glass because I don't think you're supposed to mix it in plastic."

I reseat myself and sit stiffly while she pours the foul-smelling liquid through the curls. I protect my eyes with the bit of toweling, but I deliberately keep myself from hunching, letting the liquid slide down my back. She had no right not to find the measuring cup ahead of time. I doubt that I can forgive her for that. Ever.

"There," she says. "Now we time it for ten minutes, rinse out—and bingo—all done."

"You take the curlers down first," I force myself to say.

"Yes. I meant we pour the neutralizer through the whole head. Isn't that easy?"

I don't answer.

"How do you want to set it?" she asks.

"It doesn't matter."

"How about a pageboy?"

"I don't care."

"I think a pageboy would be just lovely on you. People think you look like me—but I was never nearly as pretty as you are. You're lucky, you didn't get the bump in my nose."

I don't speak.

"I think I'll just put a baked potato in," she says.

I wait and stare at the wall with the framed sampler that I cross-stitched when I was six. I notice that the crosses are not really straight. She should've told me. A timer goes off.

"That means it's time," she says and hurries over to me. I can feel her unwinding the curlers. "Oh, my," she sighs. "It's just perfect. So soft."

She rinses the water gently through my hair, lifting the back, then the sides, then running her fingers through the front. Though I am bent back again, her fingers sliding along my scalp feel good, as if she is scratching an itch I can't quite reach. Then, as I stand dripping, she says, "Oh, we forgot to bring a large towel down. Just hang over the sink and I'll run get one."

I droop my head and see waves of hair before my eyes. The strands look like a child's drawing of an ocean. I start to cry, and the tears mix with the water on my cheeks. When she returns, she wraps the warm towel around my head and face and I turn away from her.

When I finally remove the towel, she says, "Your eyes are red. Did you get something in them?"

"I hope not."

"I brought the curlers down—the large ones," she says, smiling. She has forgotten the metal clips.

"How could you . . ." I begin.

She continues to smile, waiting.

I want to say, how could you forget the measuring cup? But my throat is closing again. She is always so sure . . . and she's going to be so wrong. I run my fingers through my hair, then hold it out to her like an offering. "It's frizzy," I say. "You made it frizzy because you don't listen. You don't read directions. You have to take test curls! It says so! But you just act like you know because you don't care. You really don't care!"

Her smile is almost gone, replaced by a dazed look. I am sobbing, pulling the hair as hard as I can as if to straighten it, when the phone rings.

"It isn't anybody!" I shout as I run to the phone.

It's Beverly. Her date's cousin is in town. She blares the usual statistics at me, half begging, half implying she's doing me a big favor. I put my hand over the receiver and call out, "It's Beverly. She wants to fix me up."

No answer. I press harder on the receiver. "Mother?" I call again. Hearing a slight rustle, I wait, but all is silent. I clear my throat to control its quaver. "Well," I bleat into that terrible void, "should I go?"

To Tell You the Truth

The week before my wedding in November 1950, my mother warns me about my Brooklyn grandmother. "Don't be hurt by anything Grandma Rae says," she murmurs through the pins in her mouth, "and stand still." She's trying to finish the hem on my going-away suit.

"What will she say?" I try not to squirm, but standing on the dining room table is making me queasy.

She removes a few pins. "Oh, she'll find fault with something—your dress, the food—it's just her way. She'll start out with, 'I have to tell you the truth.'"

"But you and Dad always say I'm just like her."

She spits out the rest of the pins. "All we mean is, she always speaks her mind."

"So?"

"Well, sweetheart, you pretty well say whatever you're thinking, too." Being the Queen of Tact, she adds, "Which is really good. We always know where we stand."

I figure she's just steeling herself against any criticism, because she's in charge of the wedding plans. My job had been to do the invitations until four months ago, when I'd burst into tears because there'd be twice as many guests from my fiancé's family as from mine. "It's not fair," I'd sobbed. "You're paying for the dinner, the reception—everything."

"It's not Ben's fault," Dad had chimed in, looking up from his newspaper. "Most of Ben's family lives here in Cincinnati."

"But even his aunts and uncles in Iowa accepted." My tone implied a gross breach of etiquette. "And on top of that, his sister is going to be my Matron of Honor. Thanks to you," I'd stabbed a finger at my mother. "'A gracious thing to do,' you said, and now look. They've taken over."

Dad had opted for reasonable. "After all, it's only seventy-five people..."

"Yeah," I mumbled, "and fifty of them his..."

Having moved to Cincinnati a couple of years earlier, in my junior year of high school, my family had only a few close friends to invite and all our relatives lived out of town. Although I had asked a good friend from school, and one from my new job as a Dictaphone operator at an advertising agency, that was it—except for an aunt, three uncles and my two grandmothers. My brother is only nine and my sister, four, so their contributions as ringbearer and flowergirl, while adorable, can hardly count as guests from my side.

"Listen," my mother had said, pulling the address book out of my hands. "You've already chosen the photographer, so let your father and me handle the rest."

I'd grumbled a bit about leaving all the work to her, but given that I would be nineteen in a few weeks and had never planned any event beyond a sleepover when I was twelve, and since I had no idea what the "rest" would consist of, I went along.

Whatever wedding tasks my mother still has to do are put on hold when Grandma and my two bachelor uncles arrive from Brooklyn a couple of days before the wedding. They have brought their own kosher pots and pans. Mom takes them to a kosher butcher to buy food and the dime store to pick up some inexpensive dishes, knives and forks. With an apologetic glance at their mother, whose eyes roam her surroundings with distrust, my uncles insist on paying for everything. Over forty years earlier, Grandma had escaped from a Russian pogrom with her husband and two oldest children, but she still keeps a close watch for stray Cossacks.

After lunch Grandma sits in my bedroom admiring my trousseau as Mom holds up each item for her inspection. When we come to a sheer black nightgown, Grandma explodes in a burst of Yiddish. "Don't worry," Mom says quickly. "Of course she'll be wearing a slip underneath."

Later, settled on the sofa and sipping her hot tea in a glass, Grandma calls me to her side. She wants to know what my Ben does for a living. He owns a small dress shop. She wonders if he wouldn't rather be a bank teller or an accountant. I don't think so. Then she leans closer and, in a conspiratorial tone, confides, "I'm sure you'll have a lovely wedding, Ninotchka. But I have to tell you the truth. It won't be as nice as your mother's."

I'm stunned, too shocked to ask why. When I corner Mom at her sewing machine, she rolls her eyes. "Who knows? Maybe she thinks mine was special because my sister eloped with an Irishman. Or maybe she doesn't like the rabbi because he's Reform. She keeps muttering he's a priest."

"But why would she be so mean?"

Mom lowers her eyes, but I'd already seen the sadness in them. "I've often thought that it's her way of saying, don't expect too much—life can disappoint you." She looks up with a wry smile. "I think of it as her early warning system." Touching my cheek, she adds, "Believe me, your wedding will be ten times more beautiful and more fun. Now let me finish your suit jacket while you go pack for your honeymoon."

Early on the day of the wedding, Dad's mother arrives from Chicago with his sister, Aunt Miriam, and Uncle Jim. Grandma Lily, under five-feet tall, has a round, baby-sweet face that clashes with what comes out of her mouth. Manhattan-born, she considers her family above reproach in manners and decorum, yet will announce, when appropriate, "It's cold enough to freeze the balls off a brass monkey."

"Years of living with my father," Dad has explained. "He could make a truck driver blush." Nonetheless, it's still startling when she studies my ring and pronounces with satisfaction, "Very nice. It will be good to pawn." Dad and Aunt Miriam exchange a sighing glance, but Uncle Jim hugs his mother-in-law. "You've got to love the woman," he laughs. "She's an original."

After the greetings, Mom motions for me to follow her upstairs into the bedroom. "The skirt is finished," she announces.

I understand instantly. "And the jacket?"

"I'm afraid I have to rip out the collar and re-attach the lining."

"Why?"

"They weren't lying right. I can fix it, but . . ."

"Not in time." My tone indicates that she has just flunked parenthood.

Her look says this-too-in-its-time-will-pass. A year ago, she had barely tacked on the ruffle of my senior prom dress before my date arrived. And too often I have sat down only to jump up after being jabbed by pins left in the hem of a skirt.

"So what am I going to do?" I whine. "I'll have nothing to wear."

"You still have the skirt and blouse."

"I'll look like a school girl. I might as well wear a jumper and knee socks."

In the loaded silence, we hear music coming from downstairs and realize that Uncle Ari is playing the piano again. Dad bursts in to tell us that Uncle Murray is teaching Uncle Jim a Russian folk dance and we have to come down and watch. That is the last straw. Tears burning my eyes from this latest betrayal, I choke out, "How am I supposed to get ready with so much craziness going on?"

Mom leaps up. "I have a great idea." She rushes on. "I'm going to call Ida, and you and she can go over to the hotel right now, order a nice lunch and take your time getting ready." With that, she dashes out of the room, Dad close behind her.

I stalk over to the closet and pull out the burgundy tweed skirt, first checking for pins, and the pink silk blouse and start to fold them.

Ida, about ten years younger than my mother, is her best friend. Formerly a dress buyer for Lord & Taylor in New York, she now has two little boys and happily treats me like a kid sister, dispensing advice on make-up and fashion. She drives right over, gathers up my two suitcases and the garment bag with my wedding dress, veil and shoes, and we continue on to the Terrace Plaza, a new hotel downtown. It's my first time in a hotel; on family visits to New York, we've always stayed with relatives. Now I'm fascinated by the beds that are half-hidden in the wall so they look like sofas until you press a button and they glide out. I move them in and out a few times, while Ida hangs up our dresses and orders lunch.

The hotel beds remind me of the efficiency apartment Ben and I rented, and I proudly inform Ida that the best thing in it is the "In-a-Door" bed. "You pull it down right out of a closet. I never have to make the bed. Just push it up."

"Saves buying a bed," she says. "Any other furniture?"

I nod. "Dad gave us a check, and the first thing we bought was a knotty pine desk with a green leather top. It has a file drawer, too. I love desks." I pause, then add as an afterthought, "Oh, and a sofa, and a wooden card table with a top that lifts up and turns into a dining table. With four folding chairs." I emphasize "four" to show that we are well prepared to entertain.

"So how are you fixed for kitchen things?"

"We've got all the pots and pans I'll ever need and six pairs of candlestick holders. I'm returning five."

"Two pairs could come in handy," she says before asking if I have any favorite recipes.

I remind her that my mother made a deal with me when I was eleven: if I practiced the piano two hours a day, I didn't have to help with housework. Luckily, after my sister was born three years later, she was able to hire a part-time housekeeper, so the deal was still on.

"You haven't ever cooked?"

"Don't worry. Mom gave me a cookbook." My smile has a hint of condescension. "After all, I can read."

"Which reminds me," Ida says, "Do you think you'll miss not finishing your education?" "Like I told Dad, I'm going to be a writer. I don't need an education."

"Ah." She glances at her watch. "I think I'll check on our lunch."

After we eat and shower, Ida puts my hair up in rollers and muses, "You know, your parents must have a lot of confidence in Ben to let you marry so young." She knew they had to go with us to the license bureau to give permission.

I point out that Ben *is* twenty-six and obviously mature. Then I chuckle, remembering. "He really startled my father when he took him aside and formally asked for my hand in marriage."

Ida laughs. "Ben's a mensch." We both know it is the highest compliment.

In my eyes, though, Ben's being an "older man" added an odd combination of excitement and security. On one of our dates, he'd shown me his World War II scrapbook wrapped in a German flag. On seeing a professional portrait of him in uniform, I'd blurted, "I didn't know you'd gone to military school." He hadn't. He'd been an infantryman in World War II but admitted he'd not yet begun shaving when his parents had the picture taken. In fact, when he and his buddies were marching through Germany, near the end of the war, they had stopped at a German farmhouse for food. None of them could stomach the army rations anymore. Once they had reassured the farm family that they meant no harm, the grandmother walked over to Ben, removed his helmet, took his face between her palms and said, in a mixture of German and English, "You should be home with your mama." So my faux pas was forgiven. But he did look twelve years old.

Ben went along with all my choices for our apartment until, probably because of my grandmother, the subject of keeping kosher came up. Although Ben's parents, and my mother, had grown up in kosher homes, neither Ben nor I had. He said he found the laws ridiculous and then made a most uncharacteristic statement. "I would never allow a wife of mine to keep kosher."

I responded automatically, in a tone as cold and unbending as steel, "No one can tell me what to do in my own kitchen." Neither of us referred to it again.

"So tell me about your Ben," Ida says, as we plop down on the sofas to relax.

"He's really funny." I sit up, delighted to tell the story. "After we'd been dating awhile, whenever we were saying goodnight in the entrance hall, Mom would come out on the upstairs landing and call down, 'Ben, dear, it's getting late and you have to be up early in the morning.' And he'd say,

'Yes, Mrs. Levin, I'm just leaving.' Week after week we went through this until one night, after Mom delivered her little announcement, Ben looked up at her with the sweetest expression and said, distinctly, 'Ah, shut up.' There was an awful silence, and then we heard this burst of laughter from my father in the bedroom while Mom scurried away. She never came out on the landing again."

Ida's startled look dissolves into laughter. "You never know how your Dad's going to react." I don't mention the unexpected sense of relief I'd felt, that my husband-to-be wasn't afraid of anything—not even my parents.

The wedding goes off without a hitch. Unless you count the fact that my little sister, presumably following instructions about "strewing" the flower petals, carefully stoops to place one petal at a time on the carpet, ending up at the wedding canopy with a nearly full basket. As the wedding march begins, Dad and I both struggle to keep from laughing.

Despite Grandma Rae's disapproval, the rabbi, a friend of Ben's family, is the perfect combination of erudition, humor and brevity. One part, however, unnerves me. "Therefore shall a man leave his father and his mother and shall cleave unto his wife." And the woman, too, the rabbi adds. What does "cleave" mean? Sever all ties? Who could I turn to if not my own mother and father? Who would make my clothes? While my mind is whirling, I'm also struck by the rabbi's comment that marriage requires two things: "*Chesed* and *Emes*"—kindness and truth. I don't know why that combination makes me uneasy. But all details fade in the afterglow of the wedding, the enthusiastic praise for my dress, my hair, the flowers and food, and the genuine happiness of those who love us. It's as if the event itself is saying, "See? You did the right thing in the right way at the right time."

After dinner, when Ben and I have changed clothes, my mother mentions that all the family members are coming back to the house. "They'll be leaving in the morning. So, if you like, you can stop home to say goodbye."

I manage an indulgent smile. How hard it must be to know that your eldest child has her own home now.

Ben and I stow my two small suitcases in the car and drive to the Netherland Plaza, the other big hotel downtown where we'll be spending one night before continuing on to our honeymoon in Wisconsin. Up in our room, which I note has one fixed double bed, I start unpacking my suitcases. Ben has hung up his robe and pajamas and sits on a chair watching me for a few minutes. "How come you didn't put all the things you'd need for tonight in just one case?" he asks.

I look down at my toothbrush, slippers, robe and my white silk nightgown. I'd decided to save the black one for the actual honeymoon. I don't want to admit that I've never packed before, so I say I forgot we were switching hotels and repacked in a hurry. After closing the suitcases, I sit down on the bed next to them.

Ben points. "If you're through with those, I'll put them in the closet." I nod and he removes them. I look at my watch. Not even ten o'clock. "Mom said everyone's going back to their house."

"That's nice," Ben says. "I really liked your aunts and uncles."

"How about my grandmothers?"

He smiles. "Your Grandma Lily told me your ring was a good investment."

"I doubt she put it that way."

He shrugs. "Close enough."

I get up and look into the large mirror over the dresser. "Mom said we could stop in if we wanted. To say goodbye."

"Really?"

"It might be fun to sneak back and surprise them. I'm sure they're not expecting us." I instantly feel foolish, but Ben stands up and holds out his hand. "Okay. Let's go. Maybe we can liven things up for them."

A few cars are out in front, so we park about a block away. As we reach my house we can hear music and laughter. We tiptoe up the porch steps to peer through the large living room windows. People are standing around holding glasses of wine. A few are gathered near the piano where my father and Uncle Ari are playing a duet and Aunt Miriam, who studied for the opera, is singing. Uncle Jim is dancing with a beaming Ida, while her husband gallantly chats with Grandma Lily, who is ensconced on the sofa like a Buddha surveying her domain. I wonder if she's told him how cold it is.

"They look like they're having a great time," Ben says.

"Don't they," I say back. I want with all my heart to rush inside and be engulfed by hugs, to stand around the piano and sing the show tunes my father always played, especially my favorites from "Oklahoma." To do the polka with Uncle Murray. But I don't move.

I feel Ben's hand on my shoulder. "So, are we going in? It's cold out here."

"It's too late." I turn to leave.

But Ben bars my way. Under the porch light I can clearly see his black hair and surprisingly light blue eyes. When we'd shown her our engagement photos, my mother smiled at Ben and said, "Handsome as a movie star." Unimpressed, Ben had said, "If I really looked like that, I would've gone to Hollywood." But he does look like that. The brave boy soldier who should be home with his mother.

The rabbi's words ring in my head like discordant notes. "Therefore shall a man leave his father and his mother, and shall cleave unto his wife."

"You sure?" Ben is eyeing me with an odd expression.

Sure? How could he have married a silly eighteen-year-old girl? Doesn't he have sense enough to be afraid? He was lucky to come home alive. How much luck does he think he has? Desperate to think of something to say, I blurt out, "I have to tell you the truth . . ." and stop cold. I am not like my grandmother—even though my mind is filling my throat with words I don't want to say: "No. I'm not sure." How can anyone marry without the option of divorce. No. I haven't told the whole truth—and nothing but the truth—not even when I said no one can tell me what to do "in my own kitchen." I know now, with a ferocious certainty, that once I married, no one ever again would tell me what to do. Are truth and kindness incompatible? Are we? I finally fall back on the only truths I am sure of at this moment. "I don't know how to pack a suitcase and I can't cook."

Ben lets out a long breath. (He tells me later he'd been holding it the whole time.) "I guess I have to tell you the truth, too," he says. "That's not a deal-breaker."

Laughter bursts out of me like a shout of relief. Ben grabs my hand, and we race to the car as if we are running for our lives.

If You're Going to Cry

"Can you believe they gave her an Irish wake?" Amused outrage roughened my mother's voice. "People laughing and drinking like it was a party. Thank God your grandmother didn't live to see it."

"A wake? For Aunt Sally?" Despite myself, I laughed. Propped up in bed with pillows, trying to save another pregnancy, I was balancing a cup of ginger tea on my stomach. The baby moved, making the cup rattle, a good sign. We were taking all our meals in the bedroom because of the so-called heat wave. The locals, my husband being one of them, wouldn't admit it was a normal, lousy Cincinnati summer.

My mother settled herself uncomfortably on a chair that Ben had brought into the bedroom before he left for work. There was hardly room for the double bed, with the TV set, a bookcase, a small end table and a large bureau with a couple of partially opened drawers that Mom had bumped into. But she took it in stride, as she did most things. A wake for her Jewish sister was not, however, your ordinary bump.

"It's not funny," Mom said, trying to suppress a smile. "I mean, really, Nina."

"Well, after thirty years of marriage, and baptizing three children, seems like Uncle Bill might have forgotten that a wake could unnerve his wife's family."

She rolled her eyes. "Anyway, that wasn't the worst part."

Worse than a funeral? Still, Mom's bachelor brothers and younger sister leaned toward the socially innocent. "Did Uncle Murray and Uncle Ari show up with kosher food and paper plates?"

57

Giving me her exasperated look, Mom shook her head.

"Did Aunt Gracie refer to her days as a chorus girl when she wore only a big hat and high heels?"

A sigh. "The three of them huddled together like refugees at first, but as soon as Bill noticed that the funeral parlor had a piano, he got Ari to play and Murray taught them a couple of his folk dances. Gracie even sang 'Red Sails In the Sunset,' a favorite of Sally's, and everybody cried."

"What did Dad think?"

"Oh, well. He grew up with Irish neighbors. In fact . . ." she broke off and chewed the inside of her cheek, a giveaway that she was torn between laughter and outrage.

"In fact what?"

"He sang 'When Irish Eyes are Smiling'. And yes, they all laughed."

I understood. Dad's favorite "don't cry, be happy" tune. "I wish I could've been there for you, Mom," I said, wishing I'd been there to see it.

She flicked her fingers. "You have enough to do taking care of yourself and a two-year-old." Her voice softened. "And how is my gorgeous granddaughter?"

"Just fine. The sitters help so much—we can't thank you enough. Ben's hired a manager so he can get home early, but the woman needs more experience before he can leave her alone for long."

"Wouldn't you know we'd move back to Chicago just when you got pregnant."

"Hard to avoid," I said, "my being pregnant four times in less than four years."

We both knew the job offer was a godsend for Dad. He still had my kid brother and sister to feed and clothe. "Nevertheless," I added, rubbing it in, "I think you should feel guilty, abandoning me here in Cincinnati, the land where nobody laughs."

Eyebrows shot up. "Where you met and married your husband, may I remind you?"

Typical. My parents, despite numerous examples to the contrary, including Aunt Sally's death at barely sixty, believed everything happens for the best. Just this morning I had told Ben that if my mother went into Pollyanna mode I'd explode. "Do you remember what she said when Josie was born?"

"Don't get into it with her, Nina," Ben said. "Look, your mother flew straight here from the funeral to see how you're doing. Just agree with her. It won't kill you." Then he gave me his knowing smile. "Actually, I guess it could. But try to remember it's just . . ." he shrugged, "her way of being grateful." I took a deep breath and smiled at my mother. "So, how're the kids handling it? The move."

"They'll do fine. Just like you did."

I couldn't keep quiet. "You know, Mom, you never understood how awful it was to start a new high school at sixteen. And going to three fifth grades wasn't so great either." Gotcha, I thought.

I was wrong. In a matter-of-fact tone, Mom said, "And you'll never know, I hope, how hard it is to watch your child suffer, and not be able to do anything about it."

I recoiled as if she'd slapped me. My own mother, the clever appeaser, going on the attack? Shock emptied my mind of any response.

After deliberately taking a sip of tea, and obviously following her own associations, she said, "You know, Aunt Sally caught every childhood disease with her kids. Measles, mumps, chicken pox. Bill took care of them all, but Sal was more upset about being stuck at home. She liked her job—being a bookkeeper. Though what she really liked was riding the bus. She told me that was the only time she had to herself to read." Her lips trembled almost imperceptibly.

According to the story handed down, at the age of seventeen Aunt Sally had eloped with Uncle Bill because Grandma would never have allowed her to marry an Irishman. For the next twenty years Grandma kept insisting it wouldn't last. But when World War II started, Uncle Bill and Grandma bonded as they listened to the radio and cursed the Nazis together. And Grandma stopped predicting the end of the marriage—to the great relief of Aunt Sally's siblings, who knew better than to argue with their mother.

"So," Mom concluded, as if accepting a fait accompli, "even though they didn't have much, it all worked out, I guess."

"You guess?"

She glanced away, looking apologetic. "I meant your grandfather didn't have much either. Yet he managed to trade tailoring for all our piano lessons."

"Did Sally's children want music lessons?"

"Bill, Jr. played trumpet in the school band," she began, then raised her hands in the "you win" position. "Okay. Probably not. The girls won a lot of roller-skating contests. They were athletic—like their father. And very competitive." She lowered her voice as if afraid of being overheard. "They blamed Sally for the fights they had in school . . . when the other kids said nasty things about their mother being Jewish."

"What did Uncle Bill do?"

"He was proud they fought back."

Getting up suddenly, she started fiddling with the framed family photographs I kept on the dresser. I think I always knew that my mother believed her sister's life had been more difficult because she'd married a non-Jew. As if she herself had led a charmed life by staying in the fold.

Her attitude embarrassed me, and it wasn't even true. I was two when my mother was widowed, so she'd reluctantly returned home and gone to work. Fortunately for me, my uncles and aunt were still stuck under grandma's roof and thumb, and entertained me whenever they could. Uncle Ari taught me to play the piano and Uncle Murray took me to the folk dancing classes he taught. Three years later Mom remarried and I was ecstatic to finally have a real Dad. At least the only one I could remember.

I tried again, the question eating at me. "So . . . Mom . . . this worst thing . . . what was it? Did Uncle Bill—" My mother abruptly put down the photograph she'd been holding and I realized she hadn't really been really seeing it. "Your Uncle Bill is a fine man. You were about eight when Daddy got sick. Bill left work and drove out to the hospital on Long Island to donate blood."

This detail was new to me and I suspected Mom was trying to make up for implicitly blaming Uncle Bill for the missing piano lessons. She had a way of not apologizing directly. "So he literally saved Dad's life." Saying it out loud, I realized that I'd never thought about it that way before . . . that I'd almost lost another father. I pressed my hand against the baby bulge and shook off a sudden chill.

Mom went on as if I hadn't spoken. "By the time your Dad recovered he'd lost his job and there I was, pregnant with your brother."

"Dad said you told him that babies bring good luck."

"They do." She moved to the edge of the bed and patted the "him" or "her" under my tunic. "Your father's cousin heard of a sales job in Chicago and within a month we left New York." She gave me a wan smile. "You had just started fifth grade. Then, five years later, when new management started cutting staff, your baby sister showed up. Luckily," she smiled for real this time, emphasizing "luckily," "a friend told your father about a Cincinnati firm needing a sales manager, and he got the job. But first," dramatic pause, "he read a bunch of books on sales management. Then we moved into our beautiful old house where you each had your own bedroom." Chuckling, she shook a finger at me. "So you see, everything worked out for the best."

The ever-ready, too-easy answer. Like her siblings, my mother always declared the glass three-quarters full. After my first pregnancy ended in the sixth month, I got pregnant again, and in less than a year Josie was born, four pounds and four weeks early—but healthy. And what did my mother say? "Sweetheart, just think of this as one long eighteen-month pregnancy—and now you have a beautiful daughter." I admit I went along, believing I could erase the shock of seeing the hospital form headed by "Boy, Kaufman." I'd been told it was a miscarriage—not a baby who had lived long enough to be called a boy. Ben signed the form for the second boy. But this time, sent to bed in my fourth month, I couldn't shake my fear. Having twice before chosen the name David, Ben and I pretended, if it was a boy again, to choose the name Randolph. Our desperate plan to outwit the negative force in the universe which, looking for David, might actually pass over the one called Randolph, like the plague in Exodus that killed the first-born sons of the Egyptians. I rubbed my stomach and swore I would never ever say it happened for the best. And if my mother found something worse—worse than death—at her sister's wake, I had to hear it.

"So, what is this worst thing?" I demanded, hoping it really was bad enough to cloud her rose-colored glasses for once. Maybe the universe didn't like people to be so sure things work out for the best. Maybe it tempts God to do the opposite just to prove who's in charge. Maybe my mother was driving me crazy. "Come on," I blurted. "You said the wake wasn't the worst thing."

Putting down her teacup, she said, "Wouldn't you like to go into the living room for a change, Nina? You can rest on the sofa, put your feet up. That's only a little further than the bathroom."

"The air conditioner is in here, Mom. Tell me what happened. Please. Before the sitter gets back with Josie."

Mom's face brightened. "I can't wait to see her. Such a dainty little thing, the way she picks up pieces of food on her tray with one pinky in the air."

"Mother."

"It's cooled off some." Rubbing her arms, Mom added, "actually, I'm a little chilled in here."

Give your mother a break, Ben had said. Okay. I slid my legs to the side of the bed. By the time I got to the living room, Mom had piled the pillows at one end for me, arranged a plate of fruit on a tray, and settled herself on the piano bench in front of the old upright Knabe piano. When we'd first moved to Cincinnati they had it hoisted up to the third floor for me to practice on. With this move, they'd given it to us rather than ship it back to Chicago.

"So?" I said, in a nicer tone. "What happened?"

Without looking at me, Mom began in a monotone, as if she were reciting a speech she'd learned unwillingly.

"After the funeral, Bill took me to their home, their first house after years in the same apartment. It was small but charming. Ideal for a retired couple. And Sal always had a good eye. A thick wool rug on the oak wood floor. Lovely framed prints on the walls . . ." She swallowed. "Then Bill pointed out a recliner that faced a small television set fitted into a walnut console and said, 'That one's mine.' Gesturing to a graceful cherry rocker, he said, 'Sally liked to sit there. It's an antique.'"

My mother paused, picked up a plum, studied it and put it back. She continued, her voice slightly higher. "He told me that Sally had originally wanted a piano so she could play again. But with a new house, they couldn't afford both the piano and the television set. It was her call, he said. And Sal decided that she'd be pretty rusty. While if they got a TV they could watch it together. He choked up for a second, then said, 'She'd usually read a book while we watched. You know how she was.' He gave me this sweet smile. 'Just like you.'"

I watched my mother begin pacing between the piano and the sofa, her fingers laced together. Her eyes were dry, but her mouth was working. I had to push up from the pillows to hear her whispering, "If I'd known . . . if she'd just said something . . . we'd have bought her . . ." She didn't finish. Her soft round face hardened into a stiff mask I'd never seen before.

So this is grief, I thought, in a kind of wonderment. The real thing my mother had kept hidden in plain sight. Bits and pieces of my mother's past—my own past—flipped through my mind like pages of an album. The dreams she told me about, not that long ago. Dreams she had for years after her husband had died. Waving a check for ten-thousand dollars and telling him they didn't have to worry about the bills. Then waking to remember he was dead and the ten-thousand dollars was his life insurance. My throat started to ache. "I hope you never know how it feels to see your child suffering." Hadn't I been listening? What could be worse than seeing *your* child lose a baby? Your grandson. What was so wrong about calling it an eighteen-month pregnancy instead of one more death? Covering my eyes, I started to cry. The whispering stopped. I looked up. Mom was studying me, her expression more thoughtful than sad. Then she bent over and caressed my cheek. "Sweetheart," she crooned, "I can't tell you things if you're going to cry."

Our little David arrived two months early, the day after I was told I could leave bed rest. He looked red-faced and angry in his first picture taken at the hospital. "As if," Ben said, "we'd evicted him before his lease was up." After the baby gained enough weight to leave the hospital, my family dashed back from Chicago to celebrate. We all gathered in the living room.

My brother and sister circled little Josie, making funny faces to see her laugh. Ben rushed around snapping pictures as if we were the royal family. Eyeing his grandson, who was still frowning, Dad announced that the boy looked like a bouncer in a bar. Mom, cradling the baby, unable to stop kissing his silky arms, asked drily, "And how would you know?" She and Dad beamed at each other as if they hadn't a worry in the world. As if this was the "best" that "everything happened for." And my eyes burned with tears.

Before anyone noticed me, baby David erupted with a pitiful wail. Mom started bouncing him up and down, but he remained inconsolable until his grandfather ran to the piano, hit a chord, and started bellowing, "When Irish Eyes Are Smiling." The baby stopped and stared. My brother and sister joined in. Little Josie clapped her hands. My mother rolled her eyes at me and shrugged her "what can you do" shrug.

And I blinked the tears back, willing them into the space behind my eyes, my throat, wherever my mother stored hers.

Leaving Home

Nina knows it is going to be a difficult day. Her parents, their two-week visit over, knock on her door before the alarm goes off.

"I'm up," she calls, and her husband, Ben, stirs beside her.

She glances at the clock radio: 7:46. Damn digitals. She grew up with a quarter to or a quarter after—a spatial as well as a time concept. Quarters were manageable. What is 46 from 60? Leaning over her husband, she whispers, "Will you see if David is up?"

Ben puts on his robe and sleepily staggers down the hall to their son's room.

She calculates. Her parents' plane departs at eleven-thirty, which means they will want to leave the house at nine-thirty for the half-hour trip to the airport. David was supposed to leave at eight this morning so he would arrive at school by dinnertime, but he has still not finished loading his car with all the stuff for his new apartment.

"Aren't your roommates bringing anything?" she had asked, and could have chimed in with his answer: "Like what?"

She groans. Let there be no arguments today. Let us all exchange loving goodbyes without straining them through clenched teeth.

Ben reappears. "I was about to knock on David's door when your dad shouted, 'Let him sleep—he's a growing boy,' so I think they woke him up. They want to know what you're doing."

"Growing, of course."

Ben buttons his shirt while she sits on the edge of the bed and stretches. "Why don't you just agree with them?" he asks. "Saves hassles."

"I do agree. They say, 'Nina, don't you think David should have a friend help him drive?' And I say, 'I told him that.' They say, 'Maybe you should tell him again,' so I say—"

"All right. I give up." He laughs.

A knock on the door is followed by her father's voice. "You up yet, Nina? We have a plane to catch, you know."

Ben opens the door a crack. "She'll be out soon," he says.

"Oh, Ben," her father says. "I'm sorry. I thought you'd left already."

"I'm just going now."

"Don't hurry on our account. We have plenty of time. Plenty."

Ben closes the door and turns back to her, controlling laughter. "See you tonight."

Josie, their ever-prepared daughter, armed with a neatly typed checklist with every item checked off, had left for her college a week earlier. With none of this last-minute fuss. She was the one who usually ran herd on David during their school years together—getting him up in the morning, checking to see if he had his homework. Maybe it was being a girl or two years older than her brother that made the difference. Somehow Nina doubts it.

She glances at the clock: 8:02. If she doesn't hurry, they'll be upset. She steps under the shower and shrieks. She's forgotten her shower cap. That means an extra ten minutes to dry her hair. She had it right at 7:46. A difficult day.

"You washed your hair—when we have a plane to catch?" her father says.

"It didn't take ten minutes," Nina says. "Actually nine."

She sees her parents exchange glances.

"We'd better get started. The airports are a mess on Mondays," her father says. "Where's David? We want to say goodbye. God knows when we'll see each other again."

"At Christmas," Nina says.

"God willing," her mother says. "I hope he's taking warm clothes."

"He's taking his entire wardrobe, stereo, headset and beanbag chair. Have you any other suggestions?" Nina asks her.

Her mother lowers her eyes, and Nina feels the old misery squeezing her insides. How many sorrys can you say before they lose all meaning—even become the opposite? "Don't say you're sorry," her father had chanted throughout her childhood. "Just don't do it again." It has taken her years to learn how hard that is.

She hears David's voice—normally low but at this hour hardly a voice, more a rasp. Her father leaps up. "There he is. David, you didn't have to get up just to say goodbye." His face opens as if catching the last precious rays of light, his typical expression when looking up at his grandson, who towers over him. She realizes she is wearing an identical expression—for her parents and their overwhelming love for her son.

"When's your plane?" David asks his grandparents.

"Eleven thirty-four," her father says. "When do *you* leave?"

"I should be ready by ten."

"We'll be gone by then," her father says.

"Really?" David looks bewildered.

His grandmother nods. "Oh, yes. We would've been gone by now, but your mother had to wash her hair."

David peers at the kitchen wall clock. "That say eight-thirty?"

Nina refuses to answer.

Her father says, "They advise everyone to come early, and we'd just as soon have a leisurely breakfast at the airport."

David nods slowly, and Nina thinks: To them, you nod, but if I say . . . She decides to say it. "If you don't leave until ten, how will you make school by dinnertime?"

He spaces each word. "It's an eight-hour drive. I'll eat lunch in the car. Okay?"

The grandparents' smiles falter, but they press them back into place until they have finished the good-bye hugs.

She is ready when, barely out of the driveway, her father says, "You're letting him drive eight hours without stopping, Nina? That's dangerous."

"I'll tell him," she says. But she cannot resist adding, "Maybe you'd like to make a little list for me."

In the rearview mirror she can see them blink, as if she has slapped them.

Feeling guilty, she says, "Why don't we have breakfast together at the airport?"

"No, no," her father says. "You should get back to David and help him pack. Don't let his back window get blocked."

She nods, clenching the wheel. She does want to get home. She hasn't really said good-bye to David, and it won't hurt to check him out. Last year he forgot his wallet.

She has to double-park at the terminal. Her father corrals a porter as her mother leans over to kiss her good-bye. Then they huddle at the curb, almost hidden in the bustle of airport confusion. They are so small. Her mother's smile is wavering, and her father's too fixed. Nina calls out, "I love you."

They nod vigorously, but do they believe her? Why is she so sure she'll see them at Christmas?

David's car is still there when she pulls into the driveway. It's nine-fifty. He appears out of the basement, arms full. "I found some old rug pieces," he says, "and a bulletin board."

"How are you going to get your speakers and beanbag chair and bulletin board into the car?" She doesn't try to disguise her irritation.

"You mad at something?"

"You were supposed to leave at eight a.m. You probably won't get away before twelve. So you'll be driving at night—with your back window all blocked."

"Not to worry," he says, backing out. "I'll look out the front one."

She goes into the kitchen. If he has no respect for her opinions, it is too late now. Over 20 years, 9 hours and 43 minutes, to be digital about it.

She reheats the coffee and tries not to watch his progress from house to car and back. He is carrying some sweaters. She can't help saying, "Why don't you pack those?"

"I'm putting them around the speakers—for protection."

The striped pullover cost her forty-five dollars. She doesn't tell him that. He will only remind her that the speakers are worth five times that.

She hunches over her coffee. His senior year. He may never live at home again. And she has barely talked to him all summer. Will they ever talk to each other again? Talk like two people who like each other?

She jumps at the soft touch on her shoulder.

He steps back. "I never know how to approach you. If I yell, you jump. If I don't, you jump."

"Guess I'm the jumpy type." She stands and embraces him, hiding her face against his chest. "Be careful, David. And have a good year."

"I'll see you at Christmas, Mom," he says, sounding not quite exasperated, but he hugs her back.

"Only if you drive carefully," she says with a smile.

They look at each other.

"Okay, Mom," he says softly.

"Did you eat breakfast?" she asks.

"Gee, I forgot. But I could use some coffee and cream for my thermos."

She carefully measures coffee into a clean white filter. The familiar activity calms her.

"Did you pack your camera?"

He snaps his fingers. "That's it. That's what I forgot."

As he heads for his room, she says, "Bring it to me, I'll refill it."

"Listen," he says, thumping back in. "Don't get upset. I didn't wash it."

"Since when?"

"Since last May."

He makes another trip to the car, and she averts her head as she gingerly extracts the stopper from the thermos. Mottled lumps of white plop out. She thoroughly washes the thermos, then fills it with the coffee—black. When she carries it to the car, she cannot see any space in the front seat for a driver, but David pushes over a duffel bag and squeezes in next to it.

"Didn't have room for the beanbag chair," he says, and pulls the door closed. She hands him the thermos, and he thrusts his head out the window. "Well, see you."

She nods, not trusting her voice. Then she remembers, "Do you have your wallet?"

His shoulders sag, and she sees his large hands tighten on the wheel. "Yes, I have my wallet."

He puts the car into gear and roars off.

Well. She had to ask. Suddenly she hears a screech of brakes. He climbs out of the car and runs toward her. "I'm sorry," he says, and hugs her. Then he gets back into the car, shoves the duffel over again and eases down the driveway, less violently than before.

Her vision wavy with tears, she stumbles back into the house. His room looks as if a giant moth has taken bites out of the furnishings. Pieces of clothing spot the rug. And there, half-hidden in the beanbag chair, is the new digital clock radio his grandparents gave him. It says 12:48. Nina checks her watch. Five to twelve. She will have to mail the clock to him. As she picks it up, the phone rings.

Their plane is late, her father says. "Did David get away?"

"Yes," she says. "Are you okay?"

"Oh, we're fine. Fine."

She waits, wondering.

"Well . . . your mother and I thought you seemed upset over David's going back to school. We don't want you to worry about him, Nina."

"I'm not worried, Dad. But thank you."

"And I noticed, when you got gas the last time, you didn't have the oil checked. You'd better do that."

"I will, Dad."

"Well, fine. That's all, then. Goodbye now."

"I'll see you soon. Tell Mom goodbye."

She hangs up and wonders if David remembered to have his oil and water checked. Does the time ever come, she muses, when you can sit back and relax.

Tucking the radio under her arm, she closes David's door behind her.

After she sets the radio on the kitchen table she stands there for a moment, looking at the clock. How could David have unplugged it at 12:48? He was already gone by then. And the answer makes her smile as she slowly winds the cord. Of course. He tripped over it last night—as she warned him he would when she told him to get an extension cord. She shakes her head, and goes in search of a box.

Scenes with a View

1

The "studio," as it had been labeled in the newspaper ad, was in a converted three-story stone house, probably built right after the Chicago Fire of 1871. "It has a lake view," her daughter had said. Squeezed into a front corner of the third floor, it tried to suggest four areas. In the entrance, the sink, refrigerator and stove, all in chipped white, were crammed against a short wall. To the right stretched one long room divided into three parts. In the back section, up one step and behind shutters, was a square room big enough for one double bed; still farther back was a bathroom with a drooping shower attachment and a slanted floor.

The front section of the long room—the living room—was too narrow to be a satisfactory walk-in closet. But it narrowed further to conclude abruptly with a window that faced Lake Shore Drive, and there, just past the whizzing cars, waited the silent and majestic lake.

"I could have had two huge rooms downstairs, but they were in the back," her daughter told her.

Two other windows flanked, at angles, the tall central one. But only patches of the lake gleamed through them, unless you leaned precariously over the radiator.

The mother had come to help her daughter settle in, bringing a tray of small plants, which she placed on the desk that had once been in the girl's suburban bedroom. That house, landlocked twenty-five miles from the city, had four bedrooms, a study, and a family room. But no view. So she and her daughter sat on two folding chairs, sipping herbal tea, while they gazed beyond the speeding cars to contemplate the lake.

The mother had never noticed before that water and clouded sky tended to match and frost seemed to coat the waves and obscure the horizon. As far as they could see, as long as they did not look directly down, whitened water stretched to the lowered fall sky.

Then both turned their gaze. A lone sailboat—probably one of the last before going into dry dock—rested just to the left, in the middle of the huge expanse of shifting water; an infinitesimal form with one sail burning orange from the hidden sun.

"You see?" the daughter said, her face rapt, yet seeking confirmation. "Isn't this the most perfect location?"

"Oh yes," the mother said, nodding. "Yes. You are really lucky to have found it."

2

The birch tree, originally set too close to the house, abruptly angled away from the second floor overhang before continuing its upward growth. It now extended a foot past the roof. The mother had noticed its strange adaptation about eight years after they built the house. It had crossed her mind to call the landscaper; then she remembered hearing that birch trees live only eleven or twelve years, and she had to turn away. She didn't want to be told for certain.

The day her son left for college, she called his attention to the tree.

"I know," he said. "It's right outside my window. I remember looking down on it when I was little. Then, when it grew past, I loved the leaves, the silvery color. They sounded silver, too. It's the one thing I'll really miss."

She had to look up to see into his eyes, a bright and clear blue. "How does it feel," she asked, "to look down at your parents? We must have seemed so big to you once."

"Strange," he said. "At first I felt hulky. Awkward." He paused, then smiled a smile right out of his babyhood. "But I can still hear you."

3

The nursing home looked like an expensive hotel, and indeed the ground floor held a row of small shops with gift items, some costly imports, for those either visiting or hoping for visitors. One shop sold fancy cookies packed in copies of old English tins. She wondered if she should send one to her son. College seemed to have increased his appetite.

She entered the wood-paneled elevator from the huge lobby and exited on her mother's floor. The hall carpeting of rose and garnet ended at her mother's room, where moss green began.

As she entered, her mother lifted heavy eyelids, and the young nurse rose respectfully. "I'll stay with her," the daughter said, and the girl left, one hand already feeling in her pocket for her cigarettes.

"Well, Mother," she said. "Have you been out of bed today?"

The woman smiled. "No."

"You must make the effort. It's important."

"Nothing to see."

The daughter glanced out the window, where an expanse of green lawn, smoother than her mother's carpet, stretched to the road.

"It's chilly out—but a beautiful clear day."

Her mother didn't answer.

"I saw your granddaughter's new apartment. Room, that is. But lovely. She's using your old lounge chair with the Colonial blue print."

Her mother's eyes shone. "She's a darling girl."

"Yes. She'll visit as soon as she gets settled."

The daughter allowed herself to study the rubber tubing that led from her mother's hand to the bulbous glass-and-metal stand. "As soon as you're well you'll love looking around this place. It's furnished beautifully. Each room has its own color schemes, yet they all blend, like flowers."

"And the baby?" her mother asked.

"He's away in college, remember? He thinks he's on his own now."

She saw her mother's gaze shift past her and turned to see its object. A painting was on the opposite wall, over the television set. It was a copy of Cézanne's compact mountains. Green slabs seemed to tumble down forever.

She turned back, but her mother was transfixed, her eyes staring, her lips parted.

"We have plenty of room for you—and for all your things," the daughter said. "You just have to concentrate on getting your strength back."

But her mother was lost in the picture as if she had found within that bounded world all the space and freedom she craved.

4

The house echoed the last ring of the phone as she entered. She sighed, stuffed her gloves into her coat pocket and hung the coat in the hall closet. There were either too many, or too few, to call back and ask if they'd just called. Whoever it was would simply have to care enough to try again.

She walked to the large glass wall that overlooked the backyard. A few leaves had begun to fall from the weeping willow that filled one corner.

A thick mass of bushes marked the four sides of the yard, except for a corkscrew willow that interrupted the line on the right. The rise and fall of the land made the other houses seem farther away than they were.

She turned back to the hall and the bedroom. Too many rooms to cross. She pictured the dust settling in the empty bedrooms, the furniture, rugs, books turning a uniform gray.

She changed into a pair of blue jeans, the old flared-leg ones she had meant to refashion. On her way to the kitchen to make tea, she again passed the expanse of window and headed instead for the basement. There, in the small back room filled with rusty tools and old pots, she found the tulip bulbs her mother had insisted on digging up last summer. Fall was the time for planting them. An odd time to put something in the ground to grow. Nevertheless, rules are rules. She found an old trowel and spoon and, in the garage, a shovel.

In the chrysanthemum bed, opposite the weeping willow, she began to dig. There was no sun left, but the effort made her sweat, and she took off her sweater and laid it on the ground. Her knees ached, and the back of her neck felt stiff, but she continued digging. Now was the time. It was almost dark, but she had no need to hurry. Her husband was visiting a branch office and wouldn't be home until late.

When she could hardly see her hands, she had to stop. She hoped the holes were the correct depth. Years and years ago she had had a victory garden. Although her mother had assured her that she hadn't pulled the sickly carrots and radishes out too soon, she had continued to weep over their stunted size, a terrible contrast to the green tops that had looked so thick and magical to her city eyes.

But tulips were elegant swaying in the spring, their narrow cups the very first sign of life. She had read that crocuses were, but she couldn't remember ever seeing a crocus first. You had to go looking for them while tulips reached boldly for your eyes. She patted the earth gently over the dormant bulbs, straightened and almost fell. Her legs trembled. It would be time to sell the house soon. If not this year, then the next. She would undoubtedly like city living. The easy access to theaters and museums. An apartment just like during their first years of marriage.

She walked back into the house and felt for the light switch but didn't turn it on. She looked out into the darkness. The bulbs would probably survive the long winter ahead. Self-contained, they would nurture themselves and wait for the spring rain.

The phone rang. Her daughter's voice, identical to her own, their friends said. "I tried to get you earlier."

"I just planted tulips."

"Blue ones?"

"Are there blue tulips?" she asked, surprised.

"Oh, yes," her daughter said with great assurance. "Anyway, I called to invite you and Dad to brunch Sunday. Are you free?

"Brunch?" She tried to picture three people seated in that room.

"Yes. I want Dad to see the view, and you can't see a thing at night."

"Of course. Thank you. We'd love to come."

"How's Grandma doing? I thought I'd drive back with you and see her."

"She's—she'd be very pleased."

"Oh, and I'm bringing home my summer clothes. They take up too much space."

"Fine."

While they spoke, she had turned on the lamp, and now its soft glow illuminated the round oak table where they used to have their meals, play cards, read the newspapers together on Sunday mornings. She sat quietly in the circle of light. Sunday they could ask her mother if she remembered the colors of the bulbs. For sure, some were red. Her mother had even installed a red kitchen telephone that matched nothing else in their home. "Every home needs a splash of red," she had explained. "It's like suddenly seeing a cardinal."

"Blue is easier on the eyes," her father had commented. But he smiled and shook his head whenever he used the red phone.

She appraised the room. The glass doors, black with night, reflected the interior like a dark mirror. She rubbed her fingers over the grain in the oak wood. She would always keep the round table.

5

She stopped her husband on the stone steps. "Remember. She doesn't notice how small it is. She only sees the lake."

He turned and glanced across the four lanes of Sunday traffic. "The lake," he repeated.

They smiled at each other.

"Do you remember our first view?" he asked. "The roof of the gas station and all the flags?"

"Pennants," she said. "Blue and orange pennants. We thought it looked cheerful."

Their daughter insisted on giving them a guided tour. She ushered them into the bedroom to admire her new striped sheets and matching comforter. Then she flung open the bathroom door as if to a drum roll. A fringed, fluffy rug, redder than geraniums, covered the tilted floor. "Doesn't this warm it up?" the girl asked. Before they could reply, she added, "And I sprayed the wastebasket to match."

"Magnificent," her mother said as the father asked, "Do you get enough heat up here?"

"I don't know. They don't have to turn it on yet."

The woman squeezed her husband's arm and led the way back into the living room. A small table was set for two in front of the large center window. "I'll use the chair behind you," their daughter called out. "Sit down and enjoy the view while I get the soufflé."

They eased into the two folding chairs, trying not to dislodge a small bowl of chrysanthemums in the center of the table.

"They're the color of your hair," the husband said to his wife. "Sort of gold-bronze." He reached for her hand. "They're my favorites."

"Why?" their daughter asked as she leaned over them to place a small casserole on a waiting trivet.

He hesitated. "They're—so reliable. Just when everything is bare, then boom. Up pop the mums blooming their hearts out. And every year they do it again."

"That's called a perennial," his wife said.

Her arm resting on her mother's shoulder, her voice hushed, the daughter said, "Look at the lake . . . it's mostly shades of green today."

They all watched the gently moving water. Feeling the warmth of her husband's hand, the mother studied the spiky flowers as they blazed against the limitless lake. She'd forgotten that autumn was the most striking season, even if it was too brief. She rubbed her cheek against her daughter's arm, velvety as tulip petals.

'Til Death Do Us Part

Her husband calls it clutter. He points to piles of papers on dining room chairs (rarely used, she points out) and catalogs stacked on kitchen counters. What does she intend to do, he asks, with clippings stuffed into envelopes stuffed into files too stuffed to close properly? Take it all with her?

She calls it preservation. "You never know when . . ." she defends the books she's read and might read again; the books she plans to read; the magazines unread but potential sources of inspiration for pieces she might write. The file cabinets store copies of correspondence with people she'd once known. Those files have become an unpublished history of her life. Of their lives. Not to mention the newspaper clippings of their son's high school tennis tournaments and their daughter's promotions at work, and both their wedding announcements, and other unforgettable articles that she's afraid she'll forget.

He relishes unfilled empty spaces to clear the mind. To invite contemplation.

She searches out small empty spaces for storage or to display photograph albums and collections from their trips, or what is the point of travel?

Their home looks like a museum, he complains.

A museum would treasure her attitude, she insists. Archives for the future . . . the ultimate repository of the past. Like the Great Alexandria Library of Egypt. "Unfortunately," she tells him, "it was destroyed and all that irreplaceable knowledge was lost."

He shakes his head. "I haven't heard that anyone has missed it."

"Philistine."

"Packrat."

Several years before, after forty years of marriage; after moving more and more boxes into and out of apartments gradually increasing in size; into and out of houses (the last one built to their own specifications with crawl spaces she had marveled over for their infinite possibilities); and after their children had left home and taken their beds and dressers with them, they had retired into a condominium with two bedrooms and one smallish storage room. They had sold the spinet piano, the octagonal oak dining room table and matching chairs, and had whittled the rest down to the round formica breakfast table with two leaves, one desk, two armoires, three filing cabinets, four bookcases and a few walls of shelves. Gradually, however, new books appeared; a larger TV demanded its own VCR; a small filing cabinet tucked itself behind an end table. And the comments about clutter increased in rancor.

Now, a decade later, the two of them are in perfect agreement: they've run out of space. A storage facility is out of the question. She dislikes the inconvenience, and he dislikes the extra expense. The time has come for someone to give in, or compromise, or change. But neither knows how. Before, they had always moved. In retirement, their options are limited both financially and physically.

The stalemate continues until they begin getting sales calls about prepaid funeral arrangements. Grateful for the distraction, they start discussing cremation versus burial plots as if they are simply planning another move. He shivers with distaste when contemplating the idea of being crammed into the unforgiving ground, constricted by a coffin and decomposing into mush. Cremation, he avows, is the only way to go. Nice clean ash.

Shuddering at a vision of flames like those devouring the Great Library of Alexandria, she nevertheless offers, if he goes first, to store his ashes in one of their lovely antique vases to keep her company, eventually to be passed on to their children. He admits, after some contemplation, that he wouldn't object to becoming part of the décor.

She, however, prefers a private little plot and simple pine box—a clean, spare space she can call her own. She also admits that she won't mind leaving behind the minutiae of one family's life. But should her daughter or her grandson consign it to a furnace or a landfill, the loss, while in no way equal to that of the Great Library, will still be irreplaceable.

Fantasies and Fabrications

Borrowed Time

Shifting from one leg to the other, to at least keep her blood circulating, Dorris thought that her usually pretty legs must be a fine sight by now, all red from the cold. Spring, like the brown and green bus, was late. The wind whipped her face and brought tears to her eyes. Better cold, she thought, than the budding greens of spring, or she might find it impossible to force herself to go into that immense, impersonal office with its chattering machines and harsh lights. And if flowers perfumed the air, how much harder it would be to return at night to a room that even a cherry-colored bedspread couldn't brighten.

Finally, the bus came rumbling down the street, and anticipation lightened her mood. *He* would be on the bus. At least she could sneak peeks at him and pretend for a while. Even if she didn't know any of the usual riders, she almost forgot that fact when she'd see the same bus driver and the same familiar faces on the same 8:10 bus five days a week for nearly five months. It was almost like belonging, if only to a bus. And still preferable to belonging to a little town that had known your family for generations, and therefore slotted you into a category, refusing to know you any better than a strange, indifferent city.

She climbed the big steps, but her ready smile froze on her lips. A new driver! She didn't know what to do with her fading smile, and turned down the aisle hoping to salvage it for one of the familiar faces. But she'd never seen any of these people before! What had happened to the round gentleman who insisted on sitting behind the driver and who glowered at any newcomer who usurped his place of honor? Where was the tiny lady, always shrouded in her black shawl? And the woman with the pink hair and unlit cigarette dangling from her lips? They couldn't all have moved away at the same time. Or been abducted by aliens. Maybe she was reading too much science fiction.

For a moment she faltered, but then she saw *him* a few seats back. Relief weakened her knees, and she stumbled, pitching forward. He jumped from his seat and reached a long arm toward her which she caught gratefully. There was nothing to do then but sit down beside him.

"Thank you," she whispered, risking a quick glance at him. He had a lopsided grin.

"No problem." He shrugged but looked pleased.

She wanted to continue this, their first conversation, but her shyness kept her silent and forced her eyes straight ahead. She was almost ashamed of herself for the ripple of joy that had warmed her at the touch of his hand. He didn't say anything further either. Well, why should he, she scolded herself. *He* didn't need to make friends with people on a bus. A guy around her age, he had to know lots of women. Besides, she'd been told that she looked cold and unapproachable. A matter of bone structure and being bone-scared, she analyzed herself with a resigned sigh. Not the type young men flirt with.

As if to prove her point, he unzipped a briefcase and extracted some papers that he began studying intently. She glanced surreptitiously at the documents, which looked legal and complicated. Memory re-traced his composed features, the dimple in his chin, his relaxed air. From the corner of her eye, she could see his legs crossed nonchalantly. Except for the uneven grin, which she'd seen for the first time today, he was a model of calm and self-assurance.

She felt a bittersweet pang to be sitting so close to him. Thank goodness he *was* here. With not *one* familiar face on the bus, she would have doubted her sanity. Still, here he was and here she was, and the streets appeared the same, so there had to be some logical explanation. People just didn't disappear like that, not all at once.

As he turned a page, his arm brushed hers and her cheeks begin to burn. Concentrate on something else, she ordered herself. Forget spring—and him. Think about—think about the bus people. Was it a holiday? Of course not. Just an ordinary Monday morning . . .

She gasped as the truth exploded within her. Before she could laugh at herself, an even greater realization made her heart pound. As if a film clip of his life were passing before her, she suddenly knew how her seat companion spent his weekends—*this* weekend anyway; that he, too, had few friends, no television set, a lonely room somewhere. She saw, with rising excitement, that he had spent Sunday walking in the park, or at some museum—but not by a radio. She pictured him reading books or business papers—but no newspaper—during this weekend . . . and possibly other weekends. Obviously he was as out of touch with this large city as she was. And, yes, that odd grin had held relief and tentative friendliness.

For a moment, Dorris hugged her joy to herself. Then her lips quirked, and a bubble of laughter escaped her. She dared to meet his eyes, then. They seemed to ask what the joke was about. Warmth and sympathy infused her voice as she said, "We're both on borrowed time."

He looked puzzled, but smiled shyly.

She blushed, but her new awareness of another's loneliness gave her the confidence to continue. "You don't watch television a great deal, do you?"

"That's a dandy crystal ball you own." He patted his briefcase. "No. This keeps me rather busy."

"I won't keep you in suspense. But weren't you the least bit surprised to see me today?"

"Surprised! I was never so glad—" He frowned. "You noticed it, too? The Great Migration? Or whatever it is?"

"Nothing as weird as all that." She bit her lip, hoping she wasn't going to sound ridiculous. "Daylight saving. People push clocks backward or forward around here. We're going to be awfully late—or early—this morning. I forget which."

He stared a moment, then his dark head flew back with a laugh of pure delight. Dorris couldn't keep from joining in. They were still smiling when their eyes met again, and she said, "I hope you won't get into any trouble if you're late."

"I won't," he said. "But it would be worth it anyway." He paused. "Daylight saving. Seems to me something that special should be celebrated . . . perhaps with a cup of coffee?"

As she hesitated, he added, "Mine is the stop after yours—and we're already late. Or early. Either way . . ."

She trembled, overcome by his words, "stop after yours." He, too, had been watching and wondering. Would either of them ever have had the courage, if that clock . . . ? A new part of her mind imagined telling the story to someone in the office. She could even imagine being kidded about it in the future . . . a future she now felt free to believe in . . . no matter what happened.

"I guess it *is* worth celebrating," she said softly. "Either way . . ."

The Man Who Won Everything

When Steve left, right after the new year, Maxine repainted the bedroom in two shades of green, and replaced the carpeting and bedspread to match the walls. For the next two months she refused all invitations, huddled evenings and weekends in bed with an open book, staring at the television set, letting the ice cream melt on her nightstand before drinking it. She would then lift the carton and offer a toast: "To Steve, thank you for wasting only fifteen years of my life." Fifteen years of her life—from a naïve twenty to an apparently witless thirty-five. So this is what bereft feels like, she thought. As if part of you has been sliced off.

Then she dated in a frenzy, accepting all blind dates, never the same man twice. When she quit dating, no one accused her of being picky after she told about the guy who offered to cook her dinner, then heated a frozen pizza in the microwave and served it with a tall glass of water. Or the nice one her mother found who wouldn't stop at red lights. And of course the prince of a guy who told her she was too old to have his children.

One question kept burning inside her. How could it be so good for so long—and then not good enough for him? And it had been good for her—from the day they met in the offices of the university newspaper, she a sophomore, he a senior and editor of the paper. A friend introduced her to him as the girl who had won the poetry prize in her freshman year, and Steve suggested she send him some of her work. She thanked him, then turned and walked into the glass door. He helped her pick up her books, and they began dating exclusively. By the time she graduated, he was in law school, at which time he moved into her apartment to save money.

His job as a waiter didn't pay enough for books, food and rent, and hers, as assistant to the head of Human Resources in an accounting firm, did. For over ten years they proved that two could live as cheaply and happily as one. Cheaply eventually became unnecessary, and happily turned out to require its own space.

As a test, like tonguing a sensitive tooth, Maxine forced herself to visit the places she and Steve had claimed as their own. She huddled in the Coronet Theater watching a rerun of a French farce they'd seen twice years ago. She didn't laugh this time. In the used-bookstore, the owner bustled over to point out some mystery novels. "I don't read them," Maxine said, and flushed because it came out so coldly. "My friend did," she added apologetically. She even visited the small art gallery on Oak Street that served herbal tea. "Stupid," she told herself. "You were the only one who drank it while he priced the paintings."

At least her workplace was safe. Then Kalle stopped by her office to invite her to a party thrown together at the last minute. "Look," she said, forestalling Maxine's refusal, "it's nothing fancy. You can even wear an old sweatshirt, not that it would make any difference. You look cute no matter what you wear."

"It's too hot for sweatshirts," Maxine said, but agreed to go. The unplanned nature of the invite allowed her, she felt, to arrive alone at eight and leave alone . . . which she did after an hour of mostly hiding on the balcony. Having pushed the down button, she was entering the elevator when a guy she recognized from the party suddenly stopped the closing doors with his arm, and got on. They rode down in silence until, as the doors began to open, he said, "Hi. I'm Mark. And you're—"

"Leaving," she said.

"What a coincidence!" He sounded astonished. "Me, too."

It wasn't that funny, but it was so silly it made her laugh. She had a weakness for silly.

"As long as we're getting along so well," Mark went on, "why don't we try that Japanese restaurant around the corner, unless you've already overdosed on broccoli and dip."

"Sorry. I'm not hungry."

"Another coincidence!" he said. "Neither am I. But that's the beauty of Asian food. You don't have to be hungry because an hour after you eat, you're hungry."

Again, she couldn't help herself and smiled even as she was shaking her head no.

"They have a killer iced tea," Mark said. "And ivory chopsticks."

"Oh hell," she said softly. At least he didn't remind her of Steve. While Steve was six feet, Mark was barely an inch taller than her five-foot-seven.

While Steve's straight blond hair fell into his blue eyes, Mark's brown eyes matched his hair.

"I'll take that as a yes," he said and led her through the door that the doorman had just opened.

On the walk to the restaurant, Mark pointed to the sky. "See that? No stars. That's the drawback of living in the city. Do you have a favorite constellation?"

She shook her head. "I only know the Big and Small Dippers."

"Ah," he said, "that's too bad."

"Why?" she asked, a bit miffed.

"Because I don't know any either."

"Why don't you just get an astronomy book?" she said.

"Because I'm subtly trying to find out what interests we share and luckily we don't share that one—well what do you know, here we are at the most authentic Japanese restaurant in Lincoln Park."

"How do you know? That it's the most authentic."

He opened the door for her and said, "Look around."

In a small room hidden behind sliding paper doors, she saw thick cushions around a square lacquered table and was enchanted despite herself. "This is lovely," she admitted, and was glad she and Steve had never eaten there.

Mark beamed. They ordered light salads and chicken yakatori. "This way," he said, "if we're hungry later we'll know why."

Soon he was trying to teach her how to use the chopsticks.

"I'd really prefer a fork," Maxine said.

"This is really very easy," he said. "It's a matter of pressing down with the forefinger."

"I believe you. People have been showing me how easy it is for years. But there are many easy things I can't do."

He laughed. "I'm the opposite. Good at all the little sports. Horseshoes, ping-pong, the twenty-yard-dash. Especially the twenty-yard-dash."

She inclined her head, a silent question.

"When you're smaller than the other boys, you learn to run fast. Very fast."

She instantly sympathized.

"Don't worry," he said. "They never caught me. Like dogs who run after cars, I don't think they wanted to. Barking was enough."

"You were lucky," she said as the waitress slipped her a fork wrapped in a napkin.

He nodded. "I am. I always win things. Nothing really big. Just door prizes, sweepstakes, things like that."

Before she could react, he gestured with his chopsticks and she unwrapped the fork, wondering if the waitress always brought a fork, just in case. Or if he had signaled the waitress, because he hadn't looked surprised when the waitress brought it. The fork felt clumsy in the delicate bowls, and when it clinked against the porcelain she glanced up, expecting an annoyed response.

"Noisy, isn't it," he said, grinning. "They really should use bamboo forks."

Relaxing, she concentrated on the small pieces of food that reminded her of a child's plate prepared by a careful parent. Steve, oddly enough, had refused to even try chopsticks. "It's an affectation," he insisted. She'd been so relieved that she chose not to ask him if his scrutinizing wine labels was in the same category. She understood how uncomfortable he'd felt, not being able to afford what his law classmates took for granted. When she had once complimented him on a blazer he'd bought at a secondhand store, his reaction caught her by surprise. "It's important to know what's good—style, fabric, cut. No one has to know where it came from."

She'd suspected that the "it" stood for "I" and had hugged him. "No one cares," she said, softly.

Steve had pulled away, offended. "Don't be silly. Of course they care."

Mark tapped her bowl with his chopsticks, interrupting her reverie. "Hey," he said, "use the fork or your fingers, I don't care. Really."

She managed a forkful of salad, and after assuring him it was delicious, asked him what he meant about his so-called luck.

"It almost caused a riot once at a fraternity dance. At the last few parties we had, I won the door prize. So this time, as a joke, when the guy put his hand in the big glass bowl, I started walking up to the front of the room. Sure enough—he pulled my number. But everyone thought it was fixed, wanted to string me up with the sweater I won." He shook his head and expertly snared a piece of cucumber with his chopsticks.

She didn't know whether to believe him. "What else?"

"Oh, pens, radios, watches. I've won half-a-dozen watches. But they were all too big for my wrist. Men's watches." He stretched out his arm.

Without thinking, she took his hand in hers. He had long, slim fingers, clean, oval nails. She had always disliked stubby hands or thick fingers. Her own hands weren't pretty or striking. Just small. A scar ran between her fourth and fifth fingers about two inches across her palm. It still tingled if touched. Some piece of nerve not quite dead.

"Are you in shock?" he asked.

She let go of his hand. "Just remembering . . ." She held out her hand, palm up, arching her fingers to make the crooked white line stand out. As he reached to touch it, she drew back.

"Does it hurt?"

"No. It happened years ago—in high school."

He wanted the whole story.

"Grasshoppers," she said. She crooked her fingers up an imaginary staircase. "I was taking a jar of them to Biology and tripped on the stairs. When I put my hand out to break my fall, it must have hit a piece of glass. I didn't feel anything. All I could think of was the grasshoppers getting away. A boyfriend had gone to a lot of trouble to catch them for me."

She continued, telling him how she had tried to wash the open wound under a faucet until another student pulled her hand away. The force of the water had been deepening the cut. Her mother met her at the hospital where a doctor put a needle in her hand—to deaden it before stitching, he'd said. Then she heard the most dreadful scream—more like a keening than a shriek.

"'What was that!' I asked, shocked. 'That was you,' the doctor told me."

Embarrassed at how long it took to tell the story, she began to apologize. But his face was stiff with anger. "That damn doctor. He should've knocked you out first."

"Still, that wasn't the kind of story to go with dinner. I'm sorry. It's my only scar so I guess, in a way, I'm proud of it."

As the waitress slid the door open to check on their tea, Maxine noticed a couple leaving another cubicle. They looked to be in their late forties. The man was wearing a leather vest over a shirt unbuttoned almost to his waist and a medallion on a chain around his neck. The woman had on a severely tailored black suit. Mark followed her gaze.

"What do you think?" he asked.

"It'll never last."

He craned his neck. "Well," he mused, "they probably don't *shop* together."

She had taken a sip of tea and began to laugh and cough. Through her napkin, she finally said, "If you're going to make me laugh, signal first so I can swallow."

"How do I know if you're going to laugh?"

Suppressing a giggle that turned into another cough, she managed a hoarse, "Stop it—you're doing it again!" After he had remained pointedly quiet for a few minutes, she asked, "Do Japanese restaurants serve fortune cookies?"

The summoned waitress looked distressed. "No fortu-nate cookies," she said.

"Do you like to eat them or just read them?" Mark asked.

"Both."

He hunched his shoulders. "Ick. They taste like manila envelopes."

"You're not supposed to eat the *fortune*," she said. "But I would think you'd like them—the element of magic, like your winning things."

He raised his dark eyebrows. "That's not magic."

"What would you call it?"

His eyes took on a faraway cast. She liked his having the composure to wait for an answer to come, letting the silence grow. And she, in turn, didn't experience his silence as a barrier, or an emptiness she had to fill. It was more like a mound of snow or clean hay, something to sink into.

"Ready?" he asked.

With his gaze focused on her, she prepared to laugh. "Ready."

"The feeling I'm going to win is a kind of certainty." He paused. "Like love. It isn't magic because it's real."

She squeezed her fingers into her scarred palm. If good luck existed, then bad luck did, too.

Her thoughts must have altered her expression because he said, "You're associating luck with losing, aren't you." His tone was sympathetic. "I won my spending money in college playing ping-pong. But that wasn't luck. Skill entered into it."

"Maybe luck is that there was always an idiot willing to play against you," she said. "I, on the other hand, was always picked last in gym. My classmates weren't fools."

"You mean you didn't play baseball?" He put on his astonished expression.

"Didn't even watch it. Don't tell me you win at baseball, too?"

"You're a crazy combination," he said.

Here it comes, she thought. Another winner who thinks everyone else is a loser.

He pointed a chopstick at her. "A human resources maven—you majored in psychology, right?"—she nodded—"who believes in fortune cookies. You don't believe in luck, but I bet you read horoscope columns."

She pointed out that astrology wasn't a matter of luck. "There's a history and a science behind it. Laws of the universe."

"And by winning, I'm breaking the law of probability, right? Probably your favorite law."

"If things can go wrong, they will." The words just popped into her head and out of her mouth. It wasn't funny anymore.

He still waved the chopstick, teasingly. "As soon as I get back from New York, I'll show you another law of probability eat the dust. I'll take you to a game the Cubs will actually win."

"What's in New York?" she asked.

"My first buying trip. I was promoted to manager for a chain of sporting goods stores, which includes a trip to prepare for their winter line. I'm supposed to know something about everything from bowling to backpacking."

"Do you?"

"I can bowl. Played Little League. I've never been hunting or fishing or backpacking."

"What will you do if someone asks your advice?"

"Get very nervous." His expression sobered. "So what went wrong?"

She shook her head, confused.

"You said, if things can go wrong, they will. What went wrong?"

He's too good a listener, she thought, then answered reluctantly. "I lost something. Or it was stolen."

"What was it?"

"A watch. I didn't even wear it that often."

"How?"

"I've been trying to forget it. It's crazy. It couldn't happen in a million years."

"But it did. So what happened?"

She sighed. "A few months ago, I decided to repaint my bedroom and get new carpeting. It had been years since the previous owners had done anything."

"So?"

She spoke quickly, trying to get it over with. "So they—the workmen—were so nice. The carpet installers cut a section off the leftover piece to fit in my closet, and the painters helped me choose the perfect two shades of green from at least twenty-five. Anyway, I have this armoire—it's really two pieces. The bottom one has drawers. The top has two doors, and when you open those, there's a little alcove and a shelf. I kept the watch on the shelf. Then, a few weeks after the painters and carpet people had gone, I went to get the watch and it wasn't there." She didn't think it necessary to add it was a gift from Steve and that she went looking for it because she'd planned to return it to him. "Then I remembered that when the carpet men were carrying the furniture back in, the top piece had tilted, and the bottom drawers had slid open and some clothing fell out. So I thought maybe the watch fell out of the top and into one of the drawers. But I looked and looked, and couldn't find it." She couldn't tell Steve. She'd never forget his anger when she had thought she lost a ring her grandmother had left her. "You are too careless. And too trusting. You can't leave things around when repairmen come in. The temptation to steal is too great." Then, when she accidentally found the ring, by stepping on it barefoot—it had apparently fallen into the old shag carpet in the bedroom—he wasn't mollified. "That only proves you got away with it this time." He'd be furious now, especially because he'd told her the watch had been quite expensive.

"The worst part," she admitted to Mark, "is that it had to be stolen. There's no other explanation."

"Maybe I can look for it," Mark said.

"I told you, I opened every single drawer. It's not there."

She hadn't meant to sound irritated, but she didn't need another man who had all the answers. "You're beautiful," Steve had told her. "And intelligent. But I have street smarts."

Softening her tone, she said, "It's late, we'd better get going."

As he drove her home, she said on impulse, "Turn right at that corner and I'll show you where I was a waitress one summer." As they reached the corner, Mark slowed, although the light was green. "Right?" he asked, and before he could continue into the intersection, a car without lights raced across the road directly in front of them. Mark's brakes screeched, and his arm shot out to stop her fall forward. They both stared into the now empty, silent street. She felt as if her ears were filled with the shriek of metal, but still heard him say, "Just one minute more . . ."

She could only nod and squeeze his arm. By the time the light turned red, and then green again, they were over the shock, and he insisted they continue driving so she could point out the little restaurant that specialized in crêpes, from entrées to desserts. "Sort of an anti-climax," she said.

"Sometimes that's enough."

If he hadn't smiled saying that, she might have thought he meant the entire date.

Still, she was relieved he didn't try to kiss her goodnight and chalked it up to her abrupt refusal of his help in finding her watch . . . and their near-accident. But he said he'd be in touch. Maybe he would, maybe he wouldn't. She half-smiled at an ironic thought. Maybe her horoscope would know. Luck, she was sure, had nothing to do with it.

Lying in bed, she tried to imagine what it felt like to win something. The only contest she'd ever entered was a dumb high school beauty contest. Each freshman homeroom nominated three girls, then voted for one to represent them. The three girls cast their votes first, in secret ballot, then waited in the hall for the results. Both of them told Maxine they had voted for her. Startled, she admitted voting for herself. She'd quoted her father, "If you don't vote for yourself, why should anyone else?" But the words cracked out of a dry throat. When the final selection was made by the school faculty, who chose a redhead with apple cheeks, Maxine felt both guilty and relieved. She couldn't help wondering if the outcome would have been different had she voted for one of the other girls.

Steve, on the other hand, had been president of the student council at his high school. But that wasn't luck. Unless luck meant he was born with enough intelligence and ambition and charm to make the whole world want to reward him. If anyone was a winner—would always be a winner—that person would be Steve. And she had lost him. What did that make her?

Mark phoned from the airport, waking her up. "The Cubs are in town next Sunday," he sang into the phone. "Brush up on your theories."

An hour later, Kalle called to discuss the party. "Where'd you go? At least three guys asked me for your number."

Maxine told her about Mark. "He's really funny, and sweet, but not my type, I'm afraid."

"You mean he's not a clone of Steve."

"Don't go analyzing me. I'm in Human Resources—you're just a CPA about to make partner."

"That means I can add two plus two, Max."

"He's too short for me. I'd tower over him in heels."

"So wear flats."

"I'll have to. We're going to a Cubs game Sun—"

Kalle broke in. "You accepted? The Queen of No?"

"He's very enthusiastic—don't go reading anything into it. I have a closetful of expensive heels."

"At least you have one less now," Kalle said, and hung up.

Maxine sighed. Kalle had never taken to Steve nor he to her.

She was glad Steve had never been much of a baseball fan. "I only like it when they win," he'd said. So there was at least one thing left to enjoy without comparisons.

Sunday turned out to be a perfect summer day, soft sun and breezes; even people's voices seemed muted as if one shout would rip the mild fabric of the air. Leading her up into the bleachers, Mark said, "The seats are kind of hard so I brought my bathroom rug for you." He spread a fluffy bright orange rug out on the wooden plank.

"Does that . . . ah . . . color . . . go with your bathroom?" she couldn't help asking.

"It does when it's on sale," he said. "Comfy?"

She nodded, charmed by his lack of self-consciousness.

They watched the parade of players, he commenting now and then, she nodding, accepting popcorn, a Coke, whatever he passed to her. After awhile she said, "All they do is strike out or get thrown out. Nobody is running anywhere."

"The pitcher has a chance at a shutout."

The man in front of them, beefy, in a tight tee shirt, turned to appraise them. "Buddy," he said, "that's why I don't bring my wife." He swung his gaze back to the field.

Her face stiffened until she heard Mark whispering in her ear, "That's why I don't bring *him*. But his wife wouldn't go with me either."

Giggling, she still felt the touch of his lips on her temple, but it was so light, she wasn't sure if it was actually a kiss.

Suddenly, everyone was standing up and screaming. He pulled her up with him. "A home run!" he shouted, his eyes squinting into the sun.

When the Cubs won two to one, she asked, "Now was that luck or skill?"

The man in front whirled. "Lady, all that matters is winning . . . any way you can. Get it?" He wheeled away.

Mark eased her forward. "I think the gentleman was about to say, 'the fault, dear Lady, lies not in the stars, but in ourselves.' And you can quote me on that." He grinned.

"Or Shakespeare."

Steve thought quoting poetry was affected, but Mark laughed and said, "Okay, smart aleck, which play?"

"*Julius Caesar*. And it has my favorite line: 'It's all Greek to me.' I couldn't believe it came from Shakespeare."

"Some things are just too good to be true," Mark said, and the look he gave her said he was no longer talking about literature.

They waited in the car for an opening in the nearly solid mass of gleaming steel. He leaned back, not turning on the motor. One hand rested lightly on the steering wheel, his other lay loose, like a child's, on the seat beside her.

"What did you mean," she began, looking at his palm, "about winning is like love?"

"I meant it's uncanny. Unplanned. And it can't be undone."

But Steve had said, it's over, honey. Like a winning streak.

Mark's open hand reached for hers. "I only know about myself. Not whatsisname."

She looked away. "That was just . . . another accident."

"Did you ever stop to think how many accidents you escaped?" With his free hand, he traced a line from her temple to her throat. "I mean, think how lucky you are. By a fraction of a second. Remember?"

For a moment she saw again the car hurtling by, heard the screech of brakes. Then a horn honked behind them and they both jumped. They looked back and a bald head poked out of a truck window. "You two jerks think there's a doubleheader?" he yelled.

"Do you ever get the feeling that you can't win 'em all?" she said.

It was fun making Mark laugh.

When they got to her building, he said, "I know a great Chinese restaurant where the owner lets you make up your own fortunes for your cookies."

"That's ridiculous," she said.

"Yes," he agreed.

"How can you make up your own predictions?"

"It takes guts. And faith. Or faith in guts. But it works."

She laughed, shaking her head. "Okay. But I need to change first."

He offered to come up and wait. When they got upstairs, he said, "I hope you don't mind, but I'm curious."

"About what?"

"Now don't get mad."

"About what?"

"Your watch. Would you let me look for it? Just this once?"

She shrugged and led him into the bedroom.

He nodded towards the armoire. "So this is the culprit." But as he moved closer to inspect it, he tripped over a pair of her high heels.

"Sorry," she said, "I wasn't expecting company," and hurriedly kicked them under the bed. Ignoring his half-smile, she then showed him how the upper doors opened, the shelf where the watch had been, the drawers that had opened, spilling their contents. "I'm not going to stand around," she said finally. "You can call me when you're finished." She pulled a long skirt out of the closet and left the room.

After changing in the kitchen, she sat down in the nook to read the rest of the Sunday paper. Absorbed in the crossword puzzle, she was startled to hear him calling. She glanced at the clock—at least half an hour had gone by. When she joined him in the bedroom, he opened the bottom drawer and pointed.

She glanced in and saw the silky turtlenecks that she wore under jackets, and a couple of cotton sweaters. "As I said, I looked in there before."

"Crouch down," he said.

She did.

"Lean over."

She did. And to her astonishment, pressed against the front side of the drawer, as if magnetized to it, was the slim silver watch.

"I didn't see it at first, either," he said. "But then, when I bent over . . . lo."

Slowly, she removed the watch from the drawer and held it in her palm. Simple. Delicate yet strong. It was a beauty. Relief flooded through her like a benediction. It hadn't been stolen! How wonderful. How glorious to know that she'd been right . . . to trust the rug men, to trust the painters. She turned to thank Mark, but he was gone. "Mark?" she called.

"In the kitchen," he called back.

She tossed the watch onto the bed, then began walking toward him when a thought struck her. There could be only one reason why Mark believed he could find the watch. And it had nothing to do with luck. He was reading the paper when she went over to him.

"Mark," she said.

He looked up, his expression solemn.

"Tell me—you didn't believe it was stolen, did you." It wasn't a question.

"No," he said, his gaze steady. "I didn't."

"You don't know how much that means to me."

"I do know. He gave it to you, didn't he."

"That's beside the point," she said.

"It is?"

She struggled to identify the feelings threading through her body, to find words from the chaos of thoughts. His words came back . . . it takes guts. She repeated them silently. It takes guts to believe . . . what you know in your gut . . . and she had known . . . did know. Unlike the half-dead nerve in her palm, her feelings for Steve had died long before she, yes, had the guts to admit it. She sank down next to Mark. "I think I'm ready," she said. When he simply raised his eyebrows, she said, "To write my own fortune."

"Ah," he said.

"Are you?" she asked.

"I already know what mine will say."

"What's that?"

He tilted his head as if confiding a secret. "Tonight you will dine with a gorgeous green-eyed lady who'll be wearing . . ." he paused, as if conjuring up an image . . . "high heels."

She deliberately showed no reaction. "Isn't it risky—being so specific?"

He shrugged. "Not when—"

Squeezing closer, she chimed in, "—you're lucky."

Once Upon a Time

1

The time has come to complete the naming of my son, the miracle of my forty-first year. The nurse has left the paper, and my husband will arrive shortly. The red face at my breast will carry on his great-grandfather's name (which I will lighten to an adorable nickname that my son likely will reject at age three). But for now I am free to fashion the middle name—the center—a name to stand for my unequaled joy in his survival after his precipitous rush to birth two months too soon. I search the past for a name as fresh as the fuzz on his head—a name as enduring as memory.

2

I waited two years for Larry Holtzman to grow as tall as me—from sixth grade to eighth. Meanwhile, I avoided stretching in an effort not to grow anymore myself, determined that when Larry's eyes were level with my own we would exchange one of those glances that forever mark one's life.

My rival, Margie Murphy, was tiny, muscular, and had begun to sprout in the front. She hurled herself through cartwheels and backflips, while I was terrified of climbing even the sturdy rope ladders in gym. When we played kissing games at parties, she and Larry always chose each other.

When I had entered this Chicago school, brand-new in the fifth grade, I made myself Margie's constant admirer. She had that power that determines who is chosen. Margie was the first to wear her sweaters backwards, sleeves pushed to the elbow. The first to spatter her raincoat with signatures. Even as I turned my sweaters around I wondered where that power came from. I accepted the fact that I would lose Margie's friendship as soon as Larry turned to me. My mother said everything comes to one who waits, so I waited.

In May of eighth grade, a regretted inch taller, I waited until the light turned red, then stepped off the curb at the corner where Larry was the crossing guard. When he ordered me back on the curb, my skin felt too tight for the feelings darting inside me like tiny wings. I knew my turn had come.

"What's your hurry?" Larry inquired, sauntering over.

I eased off the curb again so that we would be nearer eye level. "I give up, officer," I said.

"Guess I'll have to teach you to cross a street." He poked my shoulder. "Be back here at noon today."

"You don't scare me," I said, running to the opposite side. My heart thudded. But yes. He ran after me and pulled me by the arm back to the original corner.

"Stay there until I say you can go," he commanded.

Sweetly dizzy in the May sun, I rubbed my arm and waited for him to return from leading the other kids across the street. Once, I tested his attention, slipping one foot off the curb, and was rewarded with a frown.

Margie heard about it by noon, and Louis Ketchel, who was having a party the following Saturday, asked if I was coming with Larry and bent over laughing because we all went to the parties in groups without pairing off ahead of time.

We played a new game Saturday night. The girls sat on chairs arranged in a circle. Behind each girl stood a boy, except for one extra boy who stood behind an empty chair. He would call out a code number designating a particular girl. That girl was supposed to leap from her chair and run to the empty chair in front of the caller; that is, if the boy originally behind her did not stop her before she got away. Otherwise he was left with an empty chair and became the caller. The boy who won the girl won a kiss. There was a cacophony of confusion at first, and a bit of wrestling and arguing as to the best way to stop a girl from leaving her seat. After a few skirmishes it was decided that the boys must stand with their hands behind their backs until the girl's code number was called. Remembering the beloved's, and other code numbers, provided a further hurdle.

Finally, Larry called my number, and I raced with a speed my gym mates had never suspected. As I sat down Larry kissed me, and I felt wrapped in silk, happy never to move again. Then Louis Ketchel called my code number. I sensed from the lack of movement behind me that Larry had not responded. A quick glance to my right showed Margie whispering in his ear, as he bent to hear her. So I languidly rose, leaning one arm on the back of my chair as if trying to keep my balance, and Larry perked up in time to grab my hand. Louis was outraged at the outright circumventing of the rules.

"What are you—molasses?" he demanded, and everyone laughed, while Margie immediately did a parody of me and turned it into a slow, precise cartwheel. But as my heart and I sank back together, Larry leaned over to kiss me gently on the mouth. "Good going," he whispered and I knew I had entered the ranks of those who break the rules—and win.

We talked all the way home: about Mr. Kravitz, our teacher, who had had a nervous breakdown during the summer, of all times; about Margie being mean to me now that he liked me. "I don't know what I ever saw in her," he wondered, piercing me with a delight that I was sure could never be surpassed.

He then asked me to go to the movies the following weekend. I had never gone to the movies with a boy. Like an overindulged child at Christmas, I didn't know where to put this added joy. Then Larry kissed me goodnight, my first free kiss, and I silently promised him my life.

In the theater Larry held my hand at first and draped his other arm over the back of my seat. I slowly slumped down until he could drape his arm around my shoulders. The pain in my lower back was more than compensated for by the heat of his fingers against my bare arm. When he whispered comments on the movie into my hair, the brush of his lips stopped my breath. I felt as if the entire length of my body was vibrating like a tuning fork. We stayed to see half the movie over again.

On the walk home we marveled at our similar philosophy of life. We yearned for yet feared the sophistication of high school. We loved our younger precocious brothers but pronounced them spoiled. "They can't stay pests forever," I said, and quoted my mother, "This, too, in its time will pass."

Before we could manage another movie, Larry told me his father had taken a new job in Omaha (which I, an original New Yorker, thought was in Ohio), and his family would follow after eighth-grade graduation.

"We'll write," I blurted, imagining phrases of love that I had read. I would be at my best in writing, I thought. "And then we'll go to the same college."

Larry nodded, staring at the ground.

"Look," I pointed out. "I already waited two years for you." And we laughed at the children we had been.

"You'll get along better than me," I added. "Everybody likes you. No . . ." I hesitated, rewriting already. "Everybody wants *you* to like *them.*" I almost missed his reply, marveling at my sudden peek into the mystery.

Larry shook his head. "No one would ever guess how smart you are."

I stared back at him with unspeakable joy.

The following week, when Margie rolled her bobby socks down, I left mine up. Thelma Hart and Elaine Rosenthal followed me.

3

Larry wrote one letter and I wrote two. I grew three more inches and enjoyed the attentions of soft—spoken Al, red-haired Jerry, and, after our move to Cincinnati (where I discovered that Ohio was east of Chicago), an athletic Don. Names and more names until college brought Greg, a fine-boned, confident man with straightforward eyes on a level a bit above my own. Marriage followed, then a partnership in a small bookstore (more marking time than a career) until—finally—a son.

4

My husband fills in the first name.

I'm ready. "Lawrence," I tell Greg.

"Who in your family is named Lawrence?" he asks.

"We think of him as Lawrence of Omaha," I reply, and hide my smile in the soft hair of my son—the smile of one who believes that miracles always begin with "once upon a time."

At the Heart of a Secret

As usual, they did nothing all day but sleep in, make omelets together, and read the Sunday paper. No concerns about dinner, because leftovers from last night's restaurant meal would need only to be warmed up. Blissfully aware of her good fortune, Eve gazed at her husband, who was working the crossword puzzle, and said, "Let's never have any secrets from each other."

Jake lifted his pencil and looked up. "You mean from now on?"

That stumped her, but only for a moment. "Yes, of course. From now on."

He smiled. "From this minute on?"

A teasing smile of loving acceptance. The word "indulgent," however, slid into her mind like the too-sweet center in a chocolate cream. She took a sip of coffee before smiling back to give herself time to phrase a response. This was the first time in the eight months of their marriage—even in the two years since they had met—that she felt a need to choose her words. "Do you have . . . uh . . ." (she had started to say "a", then switched) some secrets from—before?"

"None I can think of right now," he said. He reached for the coffee carafe on the table between them and refilled her cup, then his. "But if I do, you'll be the first person I tell."

She was surprised to feel relieved. "Me, too," she said, and then had no idea why she said it. She had no secrets.

She turned back to the magazine section, some article that she could no longer concentrate on. Secrets. The word sounded like what they really were . . . lies. Besides, secrets were an illusion. Maybe the facts remained hidden, but the mixture of shame and guilt that tainted them would leak out eventually. She'd learned the tell-tale signs: a cutting remark deflected as "just kidding"; an over-reaction defended with an accusation, such as "you obviously get off on hurting people"; a grin more malicious than amused.

"The truth is," she said, "I hate secrets. "That's why I hate soap operas. They're all based on a person hiding some stupid fact in their past that sooner or later is found out and blows up in their faces, while if they'd just told the truth right away, nobody would've cared."

When he looked up from the crossword with a raised eyebrow, she felt silly. "Well, I guess there would've been no story then, huh."

He put his pencil down. "I'm curious. Why so much vehemence about secrets?"

Because . . . when you come right down to it—they are all lies. Lies of omission. Lies of . . . presentation, if nothing else."

"Presentation?"

Despite her effort to remain calm, she heard her voice rise with frustration. "The person is hiding—yes, deliberately hiding something about himself—in order to appear to be—to pretend he's someone he is not."

"Or hope to be. Isn't it called putting your past behind you?" His voice, though gentle, had that tinge of indulgence.

"But that's impossible," she burst out. "You can't hide who you are—not without becoming a distorted version of . . . of who you are."

"People can't change?"

"Pretending isn't changing." Feeling trapped, she tried to slow her heavy breathing. Why did she get so emotional? It made her sound weak, unsure.

"What's wrong with becoming someone different? A better or wiser person?"

"You can't become better or wiser by disowning your past—the person you were."

She waited in what threatened to become an unending silence. The kind of silence she could never decipher . . . until the thought came, unbidden. The silence of the grave.

"Then I guess it's lucky we don't have any secrets," he said and returned to his puzzle.

There it was. The raw truth. She would never know if he had any. An even more disorienting truth followed . . . would never want to know what they were.

Pressing her hand against her chest she became aware that the worm that lay coiled inside a secret had started burrowing blindly into her own heart. And she understood, for the first time, that love created its own secrets. And the pain of keeping them.

Barely hesitating, she walked over to her husband. "I guess we are lucky," she whispered, and kissed the back of his neck.

The Real Thing

When Margaret returned from her lunch hour on Friday, she noticed a black woman browsing at the costume-jewelry counter. The woman had inserted four fingers through a gold bracelet, making a band of it around the wide part of her palm. Margaret drew closer. She didn't see any of the store detectives around. She stepped next to the woman and began fingering a necklace before glancing down. The bracelet was now a golden gleam in the center of a huge brown fist. Margaret waited, touching other items on the counter, until the woman bent to a shopping bag and moved on to the shelves of purses a few feet away.

Margaret leaned across the counter to the salesgirl and whispered, "Call Security."

In a few seconds she heard the four-bell ring and glanced at the woman still staring at the purses, her fist pressed to her side. When a tall man and young woman appeared on the floor, Margaret tilted her head to indicate the woman who was now leaving the purse section for the "Down" escalator. Margaret and the man approached each other until Margaret could say, "Bracelet—right hand—escalator," staring at the broad back in the cheap brown overcoat.

Following behind, Margaret saw them stop the woman on the lower floor and continue with her to the Security office. The man turned once and nodded to indicate that Margaret should accompany them. In the cramped office, after Margaret identified the bracelet, the woman cried and offered to pay the girl questioning her. She held out three crumpled dollar bills from the seventeen dollars and sixty-four cents that she had counted from her torn wallet to prove her point. "I was gonna pay," she kept repeating.

"Are you going to prosecute for three bucks?" Margaret asked.

"Policy is to prosecute regardless," the man said. "It's a pain. You wait all day in court. But we can't let the store be known as a soft touch."

As the woman kept sobbing and begging to pay, her iridescent blouse shook into ripples of purple and gold. She swore she never had done anything like this before. Margaret couldn't look away from those colors winking in and out like a sea writhing in moonlight.

"Don't see how she'd ever get it over her hand," the girl said.

The man pointed a finger at the woman. "Do you promise never—never to come in this store again?"

The large head nodded and the man shrugged. "Okay," he said and held out the shopping bag.

Margaret left, avoiding the woman's eyes.

When she explained her late return to her supervisor, Mrs. Eberle said, "That was very brave of you. You never know what that type will do when they're caught."

Margaret nodded. Her hands trembled as she stowed her purse in her locker.

The other saleswomen fitted their questions into spare pockets of time. How did she notice? What did she do? Margaret repeated the story, adding details as she remembered them, dwelling on the huge fist, the glint of gold, the worn coat over thick shoulders.

"Weren't you frightened?"

Margaret varied her answers, for she didn't know the words for that pressure in her throat that became a heat behind her eyes.

The first thing she did upon arriving home was dump out her dresser drawers onto the floor. She could not put off straightening them any longer, she thought. Then, stepping over the piles of tangled lingerie, sweaters, scarves, and assorted tops, she rushed into the kitchen to put the eggplant casserole in the oven.

Back in the bedroom, she studied her clothing with mounting dismay. What could she have been thinking of? And with Leonard and Karen due home in less than an hour? She stood irresolute, poking at a slip with her toe. She hardly ever wore slips. And the half-slip was too short now. The wine sweater was the right color but wrong style—what did they call them? Poorboys. Yes. She always wondered why. And the jersey turtlenecks. Not worn in years. What had she ever worn the tiger print with? It looked so sleazy.

She crouched down, lifting an item, then dropping it. How could she put these things back in her clean, empty chest of drawers? Even the old sachets looked grimy. She didn't want one thing lying there. Not one. They made her shudder.

In the kitchen she found a large shopping bag with handles and returned to the bedroom. She knelt and scooped up handfuls of the soft tops, silky underwear, old sweaters. They were not the sort of thing worth saving. She had to get over accumulating pointless belongings. She stuffed the bag until she heard it tear. Half the contents of her dresser were still on the floor. In a spasm of horror she kicked them under the bed. Then she carried the bag out to the garbage cans. It would be an insult to even give the things to charity. She was sure she could smell old powder and deodorant on them.

When she entered the house again, she sniffed the air. The odor of cheese and tomato sickened her. She sat down now at the kitchen table and put her head on her arms. She wanted to weep, but she didn't know why.

When dinner was almost over, she told her husband and seventeen-year-old daughter the day's events.

"Damn fool thing to do," Leonard said, the creases of worry climbing from his forehead to his balding scalp. "She could've had a knife."

"Oh, Daddy," Karen said. "I think it's just terrible."

"She was just an ordinary housewife," Margaret said. "Not a professional thief."

"That's what I mean," Karen said. "Tormenting her for three dollars."

"Three dollars today, ten tomorrow," her father said. "Til they get caught. In fact, they say teenagers do most of the shoplifting these days."

Karen thumped her water glass down.

Margaret stirred her food, largely untouched. No one understood. She could not communicate the feeling—as if she, too, were in that fist with the gold bracelet. The truth was that she had hoped the woman *wouldn't* return the bracelet—or heave her purse to the counter and unfold a few wrinkled bills. *Do-it-do-it* she had felt their hearts beat in unison. She had *wanted* to see it, to catch her. Wanted to see her shocked recognition of Margaret's role.

After dinner she tried to admit those feelings to her husband. "Maybe it means I should become a store detective myself."

"Listen," he said. "It was a new experience—we know people steal, but we don't expect to see it right in front of us. It's exciting. Like a movie. But it's too dangerous to be a detective. You're not trained for anything like that."

He transferred his attention to the paper and she sat back. There was no point in going on and irritating him. The weekend was his R & R, as he called it, from a week of selling on the road.

Monday the supervisor said that she had passed Margaret's name along for the ten-dollar reward. Margaret had forgotten their policy, but it gave her a chance to recount her experience to the other women who had not been present before.

"I once saw a man stuffing a ladies' pantsuit into a shopping bag—can you believe it?" said a white-haired woman.

"What did you do?" Margaret hoped she would understand.

"I didn't do anything!" Mrs. Draynor said, surprised. "That's the store detective's job. But I was boiling mad, I'll tell you. The nerve. Right in front of me."

Margaret finished her sandwich hurriedly. During her faked perusal the Friday before, a few items at the costume-jewelry counter had caught her eye. They were inexpensive, and with her twenty percent discount would make a nice extra for Karen. She bit her lips recalling a friend's remark about the discount.

"That's why they give it to you," she warned. "So you end up dropping your whole paycheck before you get it."

"They say they lose money on our discount," Margaret had argued, but she discovered that most of the saleswomen did indeed buy something every week. The teenage part-timers put new items away as soon as they arrived, exchanging paycheck for parcels with hardly an intermediate glance at their earnings.

Margaret, uncertain of Karen's preference for a ceramic theater-mask pin, turned away and saw the expensive jewelry locked behind the glass cabinets across the aisle. She had heard coworkers deride the elderly lady in charge. "You could reach in and haul out a handful and she'd never notice," they said. "They sure don't enforce the retirement age here—if they have one."

The saleswoman was writing up an order as the customer examined some cameos resting in a velvet case. She should have put them away first, Margaret thought, trying to determine the customer's intentions. But the saleswoman turned, handed the lady a small package and replaced the earring tray in the cabinet. Then she noticed Margaret, who had moved closer.

"May I help you?" she asked.

"Oh no. Just looking on my lunch hour," Margaret said. "I work on three."

The woman backed up to a stool about a foot from the counter. "We're getting some new chains next week—fine gold. If you're planning to buy something, wait till you see them."

"Why thank you," Margaret said.

"Well, you look like you'd appreciate good pieces," the woman sighed. "And you know, it makes more sense to use your discount on the real thing instead of that cheap stuff over there."

Margaret smiled inwardly. Invariably, the salespeople took on the coloration of the merchandise they sold—or the customers they sold to. A hundred-dollar-a-week salesgirl would sniff at the woman who wore a twenty-dollar blouse because *her* customers wouldn't try on anything under forty dollars.

As the elevator stopped at each floor, Margaret made mental calculations. Karen had chosen something from almost every department, from lingerie to junior-jeans. By the time she left for college, her daughter would have some lovely clothes, and then Margaret could continue saving for the color television set she planned as a Christmas gift for Leonard.

It was a shame Margaret had never learned to sew. Her own mother had been a superb seamstress. Margaret still had a few baby dresses her mother had made for her. She thought of them as priceless and had dressed Karen in them only for photographs. She wished she could make Karen's clothes. It would be more personal. But the job helped. She didn't mind the selling part, but the constant checking in of merchandise, buttoning, hanging, zipping, marking, annoyed her. And not one piece in a hundred really outstanding. Not like the things in the Sheffield Room. Those silks and suedes would be a joy to handle, with hefty commissions, too. But you had to have years of seniority to transfer there.

About thirty slippery blouses were waiting to be hung when Margaret arrived, and she knew they would slip off the hangers ten times a day. "You know," she said to one of her coworkers, "I wish I could afford to buy all these—and then throw them all away. At least in Jewelry they deal with little pieces."

"Oh, I don't know," the woman said, wielding her ticketing machine expertly. "I'd hate to be stuck behind a counter."

"I hadn't thought of that," Margaret said. She felt somehow admonished, as if she had disparaged their work. None of the salespeople said they worked for the money, even when complaining of the pay. They said they needed to get out of the house, or be with people, or buy a few luxuries. What did she need? Reasons, Margaret thought vaguely. Reasons.

The following week Mrs. Pearson waved Margaret over. The elderly saleswoman proved to have a good eye for jewelry, pointing out a thin gold chain, the wires twisted into a narrow rope. She insisted on draping it over Margaret's head, pushing the mirror over for Margaret's appraisal. "It could be an heirloom," Mrs. Pearson said.

Margaret tucked her blouse collar back and spread the opening so that she could see the infinitesimal links against her skin. They seemed to make her neck thinner, finer-pored, to draw the eye down to her still-firm breasts before disappearing into the dark hollow between. Suppose the necklace had actually been her mother's? Heated against her skin. Reflecting light onto her mother's face in old photographs.

Margaret drew it slowly over her head and let it gather itself into her open palm. The entire strand coiled into a round ball no more than three-quarters of an inch in diameter.

"Now that's *you*," Mrs. Pearson said with finality.

"How much is it?" Margaret asked.

Mrs. Pearson fumbled with the tag looped over one end.

"Two-hundred-fifty dollars?" Margaret blurted.

"But that's fifty dollars off for you," Mrs. Pearson said, unwinding the coiled ball to spread it on its black velvet bed. "And gold is going up. Next year this will be five-hundred, I bet."

"Still. Let me see those others," Margaret said abruptly. "The ones for twenty-five."

Mrs. Pearson looked disappointed. "They're gold-plated," she said. "That rope could be an heirloom." But she brought out another tray.

Margaret tried on chains with links of varying shapes and sizes, their colors shifting from pale yellow to butter to almost marigold. Now they seemed to scream, "Look at me. I'm a fake." Suppose, she thought, her mother had owned a brooch heavy with pearls and opals, or a tiny diamond watch. Wouldn't they point beyond their value to an appreciation of the rare and precious? She didn't own one piece of "real" jewelry. Not one—unless you counted her chip of a diamond engagement ring. It barely caught the light.

"Excuse me," Mrs. Pearson said and approached a heavily furred customer who tapped a huge topaz ring against the counter.

"Let me see that necklace—and the one next to it," the customer said.

Mrs. Pearson placed the chains before the woman, oblivious now of Margaret. In a moment she turned her attention to another couple. Not until the first woman impatiently dismissed the jewelry, and Mrs. Pearson returned the necklaces to their tray, did Margaret realize she had been holding her breath. She could understand the criticism. Anyone could handle the pieces while Mrs. Pearson held a mirror, or wrote a sales slip.

Someone will steal it, Margaret thought. It's bad enough that one of those women could buy it in a second anyway—she makes it too easy. But two-hundred-fifty dollars. And she had already put a deposit on the television set. Besides, it was out of the question. Where would she wear jewelry like that? She hardly ever dressed up. It would be almost hidden under her blouses.

"That's a pretty one," Mrs. Pearson said, and Margaret realized she was still wearing one of the cheap necklaces and staring into the mirror.

"Shall I wrap it for you?"

"Oh." Margaret turned her head from side to side as if testing the necklace's brilliance, then pulled it over her head and dropped it on the counter. "Not yet. I want to give it a bit more thought." Her most expensive necklace, she reminded herself, was a twelve-dollar jet strand that a saleswoman had suggested to set off a red blouse she bought a few years ago. Maybe she was just too suggestible. She remembered Leonard's saying that a salesman was the easiest person to sell—because even though he thinks he has his guard up, he really wants to be sold.

All week she seemed to see gold everywhere—wide-banded wedding rings, rims on dishes, clasps on purses. Did people love gold for its rarity? Its beauty? she wondered. Or did they hark back to its first discoverer, who thought he had found a piece of the sun?

"What are you planning to give me for our twentieth wedding anniversary?" she asked Leonard the following Friday evening.

"That's years away, isn't it?" he asked.

"Don't panic. It's only a year and a half away."

"Well, I don't know—you have something special in mind?"

Margaret rubbed the hollow in her throat. "No . . . I was just thinking . . . maybe a piece of jewelry . . . the real kind you hand down in a family. It's more like an investment," she added.

"That's a neat idea, Mom," Karen said. "Can I help you pick it out?"

"Hey—I'm the picker-outer," Leonard said. "I'll be paying for it."

"But I'll be—"

"Maybe I could pitch in . . ." Margaret interrupted, staring Karen into silence.

"When I buy a present I buy all of it." Leonard looked bewildered. "What . . ." He glanced at her wrist. "Never mind—I know."

Margaret forced a smile to match his. "You choose it," she said. They had set the pattern years ago. She knew he counted on her squeal of surprise, her "However did you know?" He would take any change as an accusation—even a betrayal. Besides, it was just a temporary obsession—occupational disease of salespeople. Remember the leather coats and suede boots and cashmere cardigans she had never bought? So she'd add a gold chain to the list.

She stopped at the counter before lunch to tell Mrs. Pearson that she wasn't interested in jewelry right now. The elderly saleswoman was showing a tray of earrings to a tall girl in a raccoon jacket, leather pants and thick platform boots of caramel suede. Her long fingers were thrust into rings of various designs, and she was holding a pair of thick gold earrings to the side of her head where her blond hair would cover them.

"Let me see those, too," she said, indicating the gold chains while still twisting herself before the mirror.

Mrs. Pearson dutifully piled the trays on the counter, and the girl held up first one chain, then another, comparing them with the earrings. Finally, she said, in a bored tone, "I'll just take these," handing two golden hoops to the saleswoman.

The girl poked the rejected earrings while Mrs. Pearson wrote down the tag number, department number, charge account number, all in her square print, checking each thing twice. Margaret clenched her jaw. The store was just asking for trouble, keeping on a woman like that.

Picking up the discarded chains, one by one, Margaret felt her heartbeat accelerate. Her ears felt muffled in cotton, accenting the ache in her throat, as if someone was pressing the small crevice between her collarbones. The chain she was now holding was the rope one—the pale yellow gold seeming to twist as if the light moved instead of the delicate links. She let it fall into her left palm. She picked up another chain with her right hand and rotated it, glancing at the girl and then at Mrs. Pearson. They were absorbed, although the girl glanced up from an earring in her palm to gaze at the necklace dangling from Margaret's right hand—the hand closest to her.

Margaret checked the mirror to see if anyone was in back of her, or to either side. But she saw only the backs of customers at the other counter, or passing between. Her fingers began to close over the tiny ball in her left palm until only her closed fist rested on the counter. She continued to drape the other necklace around her other hand, shifting her head from side to side as if to catch its reflections.

When Mrs. Pearson finally presented the parcel, the girl dropped the earring and swung away, her boots thudding against the marble floor.

"Well now," Mrs. Pearson peered at Margaret. "Going to take that one?"

Margaret felt her pulse beat against the counter's hard edge. She could barely shake her head as the old woman accepted the chain dangling from Margaret's right hand and slid both trays into the case. Then she settled on her stool. "Well, we're getting some new things—a little different."

"Different?" Margaret managed, gradually turning her fist around and sliding it off the counter to her side.

"Yes. Some charms—and lockets. The old-fashioned kind. They hold little pictures. You can put them on these—or any chains you have at home."

"I'll take a look," Margaret said. "I do have an anniversary coming up."

As she pulled her purse to her shoulder with her right hand, Margaret jammed her aching left hand into her pocket. The saleswoman nodded absently and Margaret sauntered to the elevator. Her shoulders shivered, expecting a large hand to descend. But she could say she was on her way to the offices with proof that Mrs. Pearson could no longer handle her job. As the elevator climbed, she thought she could still go to the manager, explain, but the old woman would be fired. And they would probably wonder why she chose to expose the woman this way. Then, she could say she hadn't planned it in advance, but had noticed a customer trying to palm some earrings until Margaret had stepped up and prevented it.

She got to her floor and entered the powder room. Empty. She rushed into a stall, sat down and put her head between her knees. As her heart slowed, she sat up and pulled her hand from her coat pocket. No gleam showed until she gradually opened her fingers, cupping them around the ball of yellow light. She had done it. She had closed her fist and that was all there was to it. Quickly, she opened her purse and felt for the torn place in the lining, just enough to permit the chain to slide out of sight. If they did inspect the lockers, as she had heard, they never did more than just look in the purses. They had no reason to examine the lining. Especially not hers. She squeezed the purse against her chest and rested her chin on its cool surface. She imagined she felt the outline of the chain. She had done it. The golden links were hers. More than anything else they belonged to her.

That night she disposed of the other items still bunched beneath her bed, except for three silky scarves. These she spread in the now-empty drawers. Then she bathed slowly, soaping herself with care. Afterwards, she sprayed herself with the perfume Karen had given her last Mother's Day, and put on a fresh nightgown, the white batiste, pure innocence until it plunged into a deep U at the bust. Bringing the purse to the bathroom vanity, she shook the chain free and looped it over her head, letting it settle loosely around her neck and into the curve of her gown.

"Hey," Leonard said, when she approached the bed. "What's that?"
"A necklace."
"New," he said, nodding. "Saved twenty percent, right?"
"Right," Margaret said, her breath tight in her throat.
He peered closer. "How much was it?"
She heard her voice through the ringing in her ears. "I got it with my reward money. You know—for catching that woman." Could he tell? No. No one can tell the real thing unless they know. It's knowing that counts.
He smoothed the links. "Burned a hole in your pocket, huh? Very pretty."

She leaned away, pulling on the chain.

"Wait a minute," he said, sniffing. "You smell good. Get another reward?"

She laughed. "No. You do."

He laughed with her. "Pretty sexy, wearing jewelry and perfume to bed." He pulled her down on top of him and kissed her. The necklace delicately scratched her breasts. She moved against his chest and he held her tightly. Her thighs trembled and she felt the trembling move slowly upward. The chain burned, matching a heat exploding inside her. When they rolled away from each other, she caught the chain in her teeth and sucked hard at the links. Generations would uncoil the golden rope and say, "My great-great-great grandmother, a lady of impeccable taste . . ." But suppose they could say, "Here's her picture . . . and one of her mother as a young girl . . . in this exquisite locket." Margaret moaned. She must get the locket. With the store's huge markup, they would recover the loss anyway.

She wet her lips and stared into the darkness. It had to be. Heirlooms are never bought or sold. They are handed down. She fingered the chain, and her heart began beating as if it were being hammered into a thin, golden link.

The Little Woman

Liza agreed to quit her job at the travel agency after her husband's ultimatum. Some weeks later she had the definite sensation of being shorter. When she stood next to Howard, it seemed to her she reached only to his shoulder, whereas she would have sworn she used to be able to see his Adam's apple at eye level. Also, the hem of her slacks brushed the ground, instead of reaching the wedge heel of her shoes.

She tentatively mentioned it to her teenaged daughter, Mimi, who laughed and said, "Everyone shrinks when they get older."

When she went in for her six month check-up she asked to have her height measured.

"We don't do that anymore," the nurse said.

"Please," she said.

So they measured her at five feet three inches.

"I used to be five four and a quarter," she said.

"Nonsense," the doctor said. "Where did you get that?"

"All my records say it. I've always said it."

He tucked his chin in. "You gave us that measurement originally and no one ever checked it."

"They measured me when I was pregnant," she said.

The doctor shook his head. "Maybe you're slumping. That was seventeen years ago, wasn't it?"

She nodded.

"Do you feel all right?" A thin line cut between the doctor's eyes.

"Yes," she said. "Except I feel shorter."

The line became a full frown. "I think you're projecting a feeling of loss. Your daughter leaves for college in the fall?"

She stood up. "Maybe I was imagining it," she said.

Howard said there was no point going to more doctors. Besides, he was paying for his secretary's Legal Assistance course so she would be more valuable to him.

Liza gave her daughter most of her clothes to take to college. They were now too long and drooped at the neck and shoulders. Her daughter picked her up and hugged her. Then her daughter and husband insisted she was thinner, not generally smaller, and fussed over her to eat more.

Nevertheless, her fingers had difficulty closing around jars and glasses. She needed two hands to grasp the handles of pots to lift them off the stove. Her husband said she looked so cute in the kitchen, peering into cupboards on tiptoe. He said she had always needed him to reach things down for her from upper shelves; she was just too independent to admit it before.

Her oldest friend berated her for "falling prey to cultural preferences. I don't mean that you've *literally* shrunk," her friend said. "But figuratively you certainly have gone baby-doll—and that's shameful for an intelligent woman."

"But I *am* smaller," she said.

"I just hope having faced it, you'll do something about it."

When her daughter came home for Thanksgiving, Liza had the sense that she could not quite see over the edge of the stove.

"I never realized how tiny you are, Mom," Mimi said, patting her mother's head.

"I am not tiny. Or I was not. I am shrinking," she said.

"Don't be defensive about it," her daughter said. "I think you're adorable. Did you know I used to be in awe of you? But somehow now I feel—above it."

"How nice," she said, but her voice didn't carry up to her daughter's ear.

She began to have trouble thinking of herself as "I" and would have panicked except that Howard cut down his traveling and night work. He often brought her trinkets and had even taken to bathing her in the tub with a huge sponge which he squeezed overhead like a small shower. When she would squeal and try to cover her hair, he would laugh and tickle her gently. They had never before been so playful.

Actually, he used to sit transfixed before the TV and say that he would love to take courses in Existentialism and Jung with her, but he was too bushed after a full day's work. He wasn't as bushed now. In fact, he liked to sit her on his lap and read best-sellers to her. She simply hadn't the strength to lift the pages. Even paperbacks seemed thicker than her arms.

She idly wondered what the doctor would say on her next visit, and how she would reach the phone to call for an appointment. But it was getting harder to hold a thought for very long. A phrase seemed to echo in her head: "I . . . want . . ." but it trickled away and finally, as she curled on the pillow next to Howard's snoring, she could manage only "want . . . waaant . . . waaant . . ."

In her dreams there is always a tiny woman. The tiny woman sits in her husband's palm. She has the feeling his fingers are aching to close. One day he leaves their huge house. The tiny woman reaches only to the keyhole. She cleans it and polishes the key to brilliance. She begins to clean in secret places. Dream dust. The effort makes her hungry. She begins eating onions from the lowest shelf in the pantry. She eats from shelf to shelf. But only her hunger grows.

Liza began to wonder if she might eventually disappear. Or become invisible. He can't see me, she thought, but I can see him. I can see the pores in Howard's face. He has hundreds of pores. I watch him. I can tell by the movement of certain pores if he is pleased.

"Look at me, Howard," she said.

"What do you think I'm doing," he said, looking past her shoulder.

She decided he could hardly hear her. My vocal cords must have shrunk, she said to herself.

Her daughter shortened her visits. "You are obsessed with trivial details," she told her mother. "A missing button on my coat; a hole in my boot. You don't see the larger issues."

Her father smiled with pride. "My daughter thinks like a man," he said. "Women pretend to be helpless in order to suck the life out of men."

Later he said she shouldn't drive the car. Traffic was heavier and he could bring anything she needed. She agreed because her strength wasn't sufficient to turn the wheel. Even dressing took too much effort. She gave a day to polishing the brass buttons on Howard's navy blazer. Howard's pores looked pleased and he carried her off. She thought, surprised, my curves have grown smaller. My hips are pure bone.

In the morning Liza found she couldn't push the covers back. She looked at her hand. A ring was weighing it down. It was very large and heavy. And very valuable. When she pulled it off she was able to get up. But then she could hardly wade through the shag carpeting and knew she would never make it all the way to the kitchen. Climbing back on the bed was impossible. Too late for doctors, she muttered, and struggled to lift the phone to call a cab. She gave up trying to button her coat. Even though her voice was soft, the cabdriver understood and took her to the right place.

She was sure the ring, which she carried in a paper bag, was worth more than the man would give her.

"You're taking advantage because I'm small."

"You're not so small," he said and pushed the bills under the grating.

The cabdriver took her to a small hotel. "For ladies," he said. She handed him a bill with both hands.

The room was the right size, with a single bed by a narrow window. She could just manage to see people walking on the street. She wondered if some had grown without knowing, suddenly found their sleeves too short, the air less dense. She perched on the bed and looked about her. She needed a few small items. A book, a shelf, a chair. First she walked to the small park next door and sat under a flower, breathing. On the other side of the park she noticed a furniture store. Or an antique store. Or a junk store. She wasn't sure. She bought a small basket lined with cloth. When she was paying for it, the salesman drew her attention to a mirror with a strange distortion. It's just a flaw in the silver backing, he explained, causing the reflected image to appear slightly smaller. She could have it for half-price, he said, and he'd deliver it. She shook her head, having seen him eyeing the heavy bills in her hand.

"No one will ever notice the difference," he went on, though he admitted that the silver would continue to flake off, increasing the distortion, "but so gradually, and, after all, it is an antique."

She shook her head again and returned to the hotel room, where her husband was waiting.

"You left the phone book open to taxi," he said.

"I live here. I sold my ring."

"But I want to take care of you."

"The house was getting too large. I couldn't take care of myself there."

"What's wrong with people taking care of each other?"

"The carpeting is too high to walk in."

"I will get you anything you need."

"But I have my things here," she said. "My own basket. My own bedtime."

"I need you," he said.

That was plausible, she thought.

"You need me," he said. His lashes looked damp and spiky. But his pores were so large. She could get lost in them. Then she remembered the salesman.

"I found you a present," she said. "I'll call to have it delivered."

He frowned.

"It's half-price," she said. "A valuable antique."

He carried her basket for her and promised to keep it full of cheese and crackers.

Later she had the delivery man hang the new mirror on her husband's closet door so that his reflection was the first image he saw in the morning and the last image he saw before leaving the room.

At night, curled next to her husband, she murmured in her sleep and dreamed of a tiny tapeworm devouring its host. It ate and it ate and it ate. "Waaant," she moaned. "Waaaant."

The Hand That You're Dealt

Homework

Justin dashed back into school to get his sweats out of his locker and stuffed them in his backpack. When he snapped his lock shut, the sharp click echoed down the empty halls. He automatically glanced into his classroom to see if his teacher had noticed. Mrs. Murray had her suit jacket on now, her back to him. But before he could turn away, she picked up the homework pages on her desk, rolled them into a cone, and dropped them in the waste basket. Justin squeezed his backpack to his chest as if to muffle the sudden pounding of his heart. Then he pulled back from her line of vision, ran down the hall, through the big outer doors, and kept running until he was a full block away from school.

He finally slowed, breathing hard. Wait'll he told Danny. Danny probably wouldn't believe him at first.

Every morning their homework pages were passed down each row. The first person in the row stacked them in a pile at the end of Mrs. Murray's desk. She'd press her hand flatly on those papers, then demand to know who hadn't turned in his homework and what was his excuse. The culprits always raised their hands, certain she could tell there were pages missing just by her touch.

Mrs. Murray's full, pretty lips would almost disappear as she pressed them together, barely a rim of lipstick showing. She would listen to each excuse, then bore in.

"Am I to believe that you had a stomach-ache from the moment you left school until you arrived here this morning?" Or, "Am I to understand that you didn't realize your assignment was missing until it was too late to call a friend?"

They never knew whether the right answer was yes or no. Justin would listen intently for an excuse that would make Mrs. Murray smile, those rare times she said, "All right—this once." Like the time he said his father had taken his homework to the office by mistake. Even then he needed a note, usually signed by his mother. He had asked his father to write it. His father gave him a long look, then said, "I'll do it this time. Because I don't want your teacher to think you're a liar. But we won't have this problem again, will we?"

Justin shook his head.

"Nobody likes homework, but it's part of learning."

"They're just extra pages in the workbook, same as we do in class. The other second grade doesn't have to do it over again."

"Your teacher must think you need the practice."

"Maybe some kids do. I don't."

"Still . . . if those are the rules . . ."

Justin nodded. His father didn't have to say they wouldn't mention it to Justin's mother. It might mean another fight. Like the time she looked out at the new . . . Mustang in their driveway. "Men and their toys," she'd said.

"The trouble with you, Grace, is you think being an adult means never having fun."

"I don't call driving eighty miles an hour fun."

"What do you call fun, Grace? I'd really like to know."

Justin, huddled on the stairs, found himself hoping she'd have a really good answer . . . one that would make his father laugh. But his mother had glanced over, seen him sitting there, and walked away.

As Justin turned into his street, he saw Danny waiting for him. "Come on," Danny called. "We can eat something at my house."

Justin started to hurry toward him, then stopped. He couldn't tell Danny what Mrs. Murray did. Danny'd tell Carl, Carl would tell his sister, and she'd tell Mary Delaney, who'd tell the teacher. This was too important. A real secret. From everybody. His mother wouldn't believe him anyway. When he told her about the lady with the freckles who'd stood up in a car with her head through the roof, talking to his father, his mother said it came from watching too much television. His father had laughed and said the girl worked for him.

But he still wasn't allowed to watch television except on weekends. It wasn't fair. His mother watched television a lot. She said that working all day made her eyes too tired to read. Justin could see the edges of her eyes were red, even where she drew blue lines under them.

Danny headed toward his house, calling back, "Mom says it's okay to come over."

"I have to tell our housekeeper first." That was the rule since his little sister was born about a year ago. His mother had gotten a job and Mrs. Luchek came.

"I'm going over to Danny's," he called in the front door.

"What?"

Mrs. Luchek came into the hall, and Justin repeated his message. She frowned. Her gray hair was cut in bangs and curled around her face, making her look like an old little girl. "How about your homework?"

Justin took a deep breath. "I don't have any."

"Your father's coming by in an hour, you know, to take you to the health club."

Justin nodded, dropped his backpack on the hall table, and left. He felt a fluttery sense of freedom—anything was possible now.

His father came a half-hour late. Justin ran out, clutching his sweats. His father began talking as soon as Justin approached the car. "Sorry, kid. Got held up." Then he saw Justin's sneakers and groaned. "Gotta get you a new pair. How can your mother let you wear that garbage? We'll stop after."

But they didn't, because his father had to meet someone. They didn't get pizza this time, either. Justin told his mother how they ran around the track and played some basketball. His mother silently fixed him a sandwich.

The next morning, Justin took the homework pages passed to him from Kim. He slid a couple of blank pages in the middle, then passed the pile on to Anna, who put her pages on the bottom. After the piles were stacked on Mrs. Murray's desk, she touched them and asked for excuses. Justin couldn't hear them over the pounding of his heart. When Mrs. Murray announced the next assignment, he let his breath out in a whoosh. Mary Delaney glanced over, her eyebrows raised in their perpetual arc of suspicion. Justin stared back at her, with his "what's with you" expression.

The rest of the school day he alternated between bouts of intense concentration, when he pressed his pencil so deeply into the paper he could see little ridges rise on each side of the black lines, and periods of melting weakness, making it difficult to hold his book upright. His shoulders felt permanently hunched against Mrs. Murray's voice demanding to know what he'd done with his homework. But the voice never came, and he left school feeling as if he'd been lost in a fever.

That night he laid out the pieces of his car model on the folding table. He could hear the mumble of voices from his mother's television. The real test was still to come. Would Mrs. Murray decide to look through the pages this time? Was it a one-day mistake? This was the only way to find out. He'd know tomorrow for sure. But the way she rolled them up in a cone—it had to be.

Nevertheless, his hands trembled as he squeezed out a dot of glue.

He reached for a small wheel, then changed his mind. He didn't want to make a mistake. His father had put up the folding table for him this past summer so they could make some models together. There hadn't been time to finish one yet, with his father out of the house so much.

He picked up one of his father's older models, one he'd played with himself as a boy. He'd told Justin how he'd polished the metal, painted the racing stripes, fit in the little steering wheel. Justin crouched down to push the car along the wooden edge of the floor, where the rug ended. He zoomed along, clambering to keep up on his knees; the powerful driver, squinting behind his goggles, tense but unafraid, and above all, in control. That's the secret of racing, his father told him. Keeping that edge of control . . . knowing how far you can go.

When his mother complained of the noise, he moved the car onto the rug. But the thick pile soaked up the sound and speed. He sighed and went back to the folding table. He poked at the parts of the model but didn't pick up the glue. It was more fun if his father showed him.

In the morning he kissed his mother goodbye and saw the red lining her eyes. Suppose Mrs. Murray called her. A quick confession now could save him. But then his father came into the kitchen and smiled at him. Maybe his father had slept at home last night instead of on the couch in his office. A good omen.

Day after day, for almost a month, Justin passed on the homework pages of his classmates, sandwiching a blank page of his own in between. Mrs. Murray would press her hand against the stack on her desk, but he knew the truth. Mrs. Murray didn't like homework either. He didn't argue with his mother about doing it anymore, either. He felt a little bad when she told him she was happy he was taking responsibility.

As a reward she said he could go with his father to his new health club on Wednesday nights, even though it was a school night. A couple of times they picked up the girl with the freckles outside a tall building his father called a condo. Katie had thick reddish hair, and a big laugh. Justin didn't mention Katie. Mrs. Murray never called. And his father finished one of the models with him. So everything was working out.

Then Mary Delaney didn't do her homework and forgot to bring a note. When Mrs. Murray said she was surprised, Mary was so dependable, Mary's face swelled into a circle of mottled red and she blurted, "You never yell at Justin and he *never* turns his homework in."

Justin grabbed the sides of his desk and watched as if the little scene were on a stage, every word a hammer blow to his breastbone.

"What are you saying?" Mrs. Murray asked.

Mary Delaney looked like a pasty rubber doll planted in front of Mrs. Murray's desk. "Justin passes on everybody else's homework. But he never puts in his own."

Mrs. Murray lifted one eyebrow. "Never?"

Mary Delaney's solid cheeks shone with indignation. "Never. Not today, either."

Justin's ears felt stuffed with his heart's pounding. But Mrs. Murray simply picked up the stack of pages on her desk and began, with her rubber-tipped finger, to slide the corner of each page aside. Somewhere toward the end of the pile, where Justin's group would be, she stopped. Justin tasted a sour liquid in his throat.

"Why, here it is," Mrs. Murray said, and she looked straight at Justin. He tried to focus through the haze distorting his vision. Then Mrs. Murray said, "I think you've made a mistake, Mary. I'll expect a note tomorrow." She paused, again looked straight at Justin as she added, "I'm sure your paper will be here, too, Justin."

Justin's perspiring hands slid off the desk. He could barely nod his gratitude. That she would do this for him.

"Wow," Danny said as they walked home. "Can you believe that Mary Delaney—the fink? How'd she think she'd get away with it? That girl's gone around the bend."

Justin shrugged, started running.

"What's your hurry?" Danny jogged alongside.

"My Dad's taking me to his club."

But he wasn't. He came into Justin's room after dinner. "How're you doing?"

Justin debated the briefest of moments, then said, "Okay, I guess."

His father closed the door behind him, and sat down on Justin's bed, leaning forward, elbows on his knees. The room seemed too small to Justin now, his desk and chair like toy furniture. "School okay?"

Justin picked up a toy car, spun its wheels. "Yeah."

"Getting along with your teacher?"

Justin rolled the car up and down his hip. It began to slip in his hand, wet with perspiration.

"I guess you've been wondering," his father began.

Justin snuck a quick glance. His father was holding a pillow against his stomach, like Justin did when he had cramps. "Wondering what?"

"Why I'm not home that much any more."

Justin squeezed the car, feeling the metal dig into his palm. He prayed quickly. "Don't go away. Please don't go away."

"I'm moving out—to a place of my own."

Justin pushed the question through stiff lips. "The condo?"

His father nodded, then tossed the pillow and drew Justin close to him. He took the car out of the boy's hands and held them tightly in his. "But I'll see you—you don't have to worry about that. And you'll visit me, too. I'll have a couch that opens into a bed. That'll be your bed."

Justin tried to pull his hands away, but his father held on. "I just wanted you to know. Not to worry—okay?"

Justin nodded. He heard his father sigh as he got up from the bed.

"My teacher," Justin said quickly. His father turned back. "My teacher. She doesn't read our homework."

His father waited. When Justin didn't go on, he said, "What're you talking about?"

"She throws it away. She just throws it away without looking."

His father's head tilted to one side, as if he were trying to hear better. "That's not possible, Justin."

"It's true. I didn't do my homework and she never knew. Then, when Mary Delaney found out, Mrs. Murray lied. She said she had my homework paper right there—but she didn't."

Now, Justin thought.

His father's eyes narrowed. "Justin, it won't help. Making up stories like that."

Justin's throat ached. If he said any more, the tears would fall out. He grabbed the car and pressed it against his mouth.

"Don't, Justin." His father walked back and took him in his arms. "I love you, kid. Everything'll be all right. You'll see. We'll still have great times together." Then he held Justin in front of him. "Now do your homework, okay? Don't get your mother upset."

"But Mrs. Murray knows it's true. She didn't want me to get in trouble. So she lied! Just ask her . . ." he broke off. How dumb could he be? It was her. She was afraid they'd find out about *her*. What *she* did. He tried to pull away, but his father wouldn't let go.

"Justin." His father shook him slightly. "I know how you feel, and I'm sorry. But this has nothing to do with you—or your homework. No matter what—I'm still your father."

Justin finally pulled one hand free. He raised it toward his father's face, as if to strike. "I'm going to tell Mom," he shouted. But even as he said it, he knew it was too late.

Radishes and Daffodils

As she rinsed the lettuce, Natalie gloated. No matter what bad news Max was saving up for her, in only a couple of months she would be planting, and harvesting, her own bib and romaine, flavored with her own rosemary, chives and basil. She loved to stand at the kitchen window, squaring off with her eyes the various plots and rows, envisioning the greening of her yard.

"For a born-and-bred city girl you've got the blood of a dirt farmer," Max told her, whenever he came home to find her still kneeling before her plants, tying or clearing, clipping or sprinkling. He repeated the words whenever he bumped into one of her indoor plants, often an outdoor variety being carefully nurtured for its hardier life later on.

"Who ever heard of trees inside?" he'd complain, rubbing a bruised elbow or shin. He never learned the name of one leaf or flower, calling them either trees or weeds.

But she knew from her youth nothing ever grew in city dirt beneath city feet. She had surreptitiously bought seeds to press in little mounds of dirt on the outside window sill, but rain flattened them to muddy streaks, indistinguishable from the other grime, and there seemed to be no sun. When her father had come upon one of the empty packets, he had wheezed, "Rabbit food," with the expensive asthma that had come upon him with unemployment.

She began slicing the green onions, her miniature bulbs. Bulbs were her favorites, like her daffodils and tazetta narcissus she began indoors for winter blooming. Something about their self-contained strength appealed to her. Their food for survival locked in, hidden, waiting for the moment of blossoming. Then dying to survive again.

She jumped as Max entered the kitchen. "I didn't hear . . ." she began. But his eyes flickered away from hers as he mumbled something and walked past her into the family room. She began mindlessly slicing the radishes, deliberately focusing her attention on the rocking blade and smooth maple block. Something had been wrong for weeks, but it would have done no good to ask. "No point both of us being upset" was all he'd ever say until some crisis—usually minor in retrospect—had passed.

She waited until he slumped in a corner of the sofa with his martini. Then she pulled the ottoman over to sit in front of him.

"Do you want . . ." she began, but he didn't need more encouragement, and the part of her that had learned to interpret his signs gave thanks that the children were staying overnight with friends.

"It's all over," he said flatly. "Finished. Kaput."

He usually began with hyperbole, but the little nervous laugh was missing, the laugh that was supposed to mean, I'm exaggerating but not by much. She felt a hollowing begin within her.

"Another month and I'm officially terminated—how do you like that for aptness? Officially terminated—tossed out—given a few months to live—on what they call separation pay. Hell. They should've killed me outright. The insurance policy they pay on me—that $100,000—is a better deal. But that'll go, too."

He drank deeply, then put the glass on the table . . . no coaster . . . a small attack on the house.

She breathed shallowly, as if holding herself in some fragile shell that could be shattered by even a caught sob. She gently licked her lips. "What," she began softly, "what are you . . ." she paused, "planning to do?"

"Do? Do? What do you think I've been doing the past two months?" He waved his hand. "Trying to spare you. No point getting you hysterical. I've gone on a thousand interviews. There are no jobs. No jobs that will support *this* house—and acreage." He jerked his head, but his look accused her. "That's the first thing we have to do. Sell this place."

She didn't allow her eyes to stray from his face to the walls, glass doors—not even to the delicate birch, sentinel to the patio. She didn't need her eyes anyway. Her hands remembered rubbing the gleam into dark panels and surfaces. The scent of her plants, the moist dirt, was always in her nostrils, their textures under the pads of her fingers. She wore garden gloves reluctantly—removing them now and then to pat the ground or stroke a feathery leaf. But he knew this.

Instead she whispered, "The children," and regretted it. No time for old battles. But he had caught the whisper—had probably been waiting for it.

"They'll get jobs after school. If they want to go to college, they'll have to hustle. Like I did. Won't hurt them. Be good for them. Plenty do it. They could use lessons in earning money for a change."

Lessons. The red flag. He had never had tennis lessons, skating lessons, voice lessons. A person wants to play a game or sing—he said—they just do it. A logic she couldn't attack, since it was based on his satisfaction—supposed satisfaction—with himself. He might brag about Jamie's perfect tennis strokes, or Carol's leads in school musicals. But he called it talent, believed talent will out, like a dropped seed will sprout. Nurturing? Developing? Protection from trampling? No. She mustn't think in that direction yet.

"Maybe I—could do something," she ventured.

"*You?* You think a salesgirl can support a family? A receptionist? Even a farmer?" He smiled briefly.

Ah. She welcomed the old anger. It stiffened her, straightened her back, strengthened her voice. The perfect housewife and mother. What did she need a part-time job for? He liked her to be home when he got there. Why have a beautiful home with no one in it all day long? When she had joined the gardening club he had laughed with derisive satisfaction. "Leave it to a woman to get a hobby that costs a fortune. Any hired foreigner could do it for less."

"When I grow our own food, you'll choke laughing—with your mouth full."

"I bet your tomatoes will cost twice what the store charges," he'd replied. And they had. So he was right again. She could never earn enough. Never.

He was smiling his tight, annoyed smile, and her anger gave way to panic. Was he really finished? Was he going to give up? He knew the situation better than she did. What could she say? Again she licked her lips, but her tongue caught at their dryness. She realized she had been breathing with her mouth open—short, shallow breaths.

"God knows where we'll live," he continued. "We can't stay in the suburbs, that's for sure. An apartment in the city." He seemed to relish throwing the words at her, as if saying, Yes—I hit the mark that time. He knew she was terrified of the city. But she must remember—he was frightened, too. He had gotten his position through a cousin, long since dead. He didn't like to be reminded of it, but surely it was eating at him now.

"There're inexpensive houses," she began, but that wasn't the point. You can't go back again—keep the same friends. She had seen it before.

Sympathy at first. Then avoidance. Embarrassment at mentioning their vacations, their cars, their furs. Then resentment at having to censor their language, their enthusiasms. Then believing they see envy, accusation shading the voice, shadowing the eyes, pleading, Why me and not you?

As if he ran along her train of thought, he added, "Won't see too many of our friends in the city." He was beginning already. "One advantage, though—a small place will be easier for you, without help. You could never take care of a house this size alone." Another bullseye. He had given her everything, and he had the power to take it away.

The panic had reached her throat. She was near screaming, You cheat! You fraud! You talk big-man protection, self-made, and now you'll fall and take us all down with you. He had already abdicated. Was already leaning. She would get a job. Any job. And he would sneer at it, compared to what he had once brought home. Proof, weekly, of his gifts, superior to hers. He would accept the children's sacrifices, in the name of a healthy offering. An offering owed in return for original life. He would bloat on a chair, his veins spreading in his face. And by the time he died it would do no one any good. Leave nothing but a faint relief, a metallic taste of shame and guilt. She had seen it before. She had only to look at her own soft hands, even when grimy with good dirt, to see her mother's red, swollen fingers, never still, jerking even in sleep.

"Stay in school," her mother had begged, knowing it was impossible. Knowing her daughter's only way out of those dark, molting rooms, with their peeling paper and scarred plaster, was with a job and a chance to meet someone stronger than the flabby father whose muscles couldn't fight bad luck. Death delayed was death prayed for.

She stood abruptly and returned to the kitchen, to her window, to her green expectations. The bulbs, already in the ground, waited. So near their time. She could feel their readiness to burst from darkness. But others she had "forced" indoors. Pampered to bloom. Created special conditions for them. Timing was all. She needed only time. No time to think. Only to act.

"How long you going to stare out the window?" He sounded aggrieved. "Weren't you making a salad when I came in?"

"Yes. The children won't be here for dinner." She automatically opened the door of the refrigerator. The salad fixings lay wrapped neatly in the plastic vegetable bin. But she was seeing her bulbs, waiting below. Her lovely lily of the valley, her autumn crocus, her daffodils. She had kept some indoors for forcing—to have blooms all winter long. Strange that with such beauty they were so poisonous. She had warned the children never to eat any bulb from the garden, for fear they would choose the deadly daffodil as well as the radish.

"I thought I'd make us a special salad," she said abruptly, shutting the refrigerator door. "With lots of the anchovies you like." She hurried to the basement to gather her new ingredients before he might notice her trembling. She could feel the heat in her cheeks and was surprised at her excitement. Knowledge *was* power. Even knowledge lying dormant, like the bulbs, waiting to be forced into the light.

Santa Claus Is a Man

Robby thrust his face up into the bite of the wind, imagining he could smell pine from the trees gleaming through apartment windows. Narrowing his eyes to make a blur of the multi-colored lights strung through the bushes, he spurted into a half-trot. He could say he was kept after. You'd think they could cancel Hebrew classes, particularly on top of Christmas vacation.

He scooped a palmful of snow from a laden hedge and threw it, without packing it into a snowball. Well, it didn't matter anyway. He wasn't going back.

He pulled open the heavy outer door, used his key in the vestibule door rather than buzz the apartment, and took the steps in pairs. He swung past the Boyd door with its pointy red-and-green wreath, and nodded as if agreement had been found. On the second floor, he pushed his key into the lock, leaning heavily on the door so that he nearly fell as it opened into the narrow hallway. His mother darted around the corner from the kitchen, her lips parted.

"Don't," Robby barked. "I was kept after."

"At Xavier's gym?" His mother's eyes moved slightly to the left. "Hebrew school is *that* way, I believe."

Had she called the school? He abandoned his plan to wait for the right moment, as if he had planned it originally for his mother's sake. "I've decided not to be bar mitzvahed anyway."

"Take off your coat. Dinner in five minutes." His mother whirled back to the kitchen.

By the squeezed-out sound of her words, Robby knew she was controlling herself.

He stuffed his coat in the closet before following her into the kitchen. "You said everyone should be treated with respect. You said even children have rights."

"So now we know what I said. And what did you say?"

He peered into the refrigerator. "I said I didn't want the blessing. Then the rabbi said if I didn't want the blessing, don't come up to the bema—"

"Sit down," his mother said, shutting the refrigerator door so that Robby had to jump backwards.

As he slid into his chair, she said, "By the way, Mrs. Boyd would like you to watch Kevin tomorrow morning. She has some last-minute shopping, after being stuck inside all week with the flu."

He ate automatically, not tasting the food. She was probably thinking, "We'll wait 'til vacation is over." He hated that. Waiting felt like a fist in his stomach. He'd rather be punished, get it over. Mostly, he wanted to stop her before she said, "Your father would have wanted . . ."

"I can't go back," he said. "It's different now."

"I need time to think, Robby. You had time, didn't you?"

He had no more words. When he refused dessert, they cleared the table and did the dishes in silence. Then she let him escape to his room.

He pretended he didn't hear the soft knock. "Robby?" His door opened a crack. He stiffened.

"Shall I tell Mrs. Boyd it's okay? She'll have Kevin dressed and ready to go out."

He tossed his catcher's mitt from hand to hand. "All right."

In the morning, he stayed in bed until his mother knocked and warned him he'd be late and he still had to eat breakfast.

As he swallowed his toast, his mother led in Kevin, who stood like a stuffed animal in his quilted snowsuit. The boy's blue eyes widened in a way that embarrassed Robby, but still felt good. He knew his mother was right when she said the kindergartner thought Robby was God himself. He threw his coat on and guided Kevin down the stairs, nodding to his mother's admonishments as she followed them out to the landing.

"How about the swing park, Kev? Up in the old air," Robby said, pushing open the big door downstairs.

"I want to see Santa Claus."

Robby patted Kevin through the doorway and sniffed the cold air. "Come on now, Kev. Maybe you'll touch the sky this time."

"First Santa Claus."

"Don't be silly." Robby began striding ahead. An unholy wail made him swivel. Kevin still stood in front of the door, his sausage arms hanging, tears pouring in a torrent.

Robby rushed back and dabbed at the little face with his glove. "Calm down, don't cry," he muttered, keeping up a stream of words. When Kevin finally slowed to hiccoughing, Robby gripped the child's shoulder. "What's the matter with you? What kind of way is that to act?"

Kevin stared up, his expression imploring.

"Wipe your nose—use your mitten. Come on."

"I have to see him," Kevin said. "By myself."

"Kids don't ever see him alone," Robby said carefully, thinking that's what they meant by precocious.

"I *have* to see him," Kevin repeated and looked as if he was about to unleash another wail.

"Now just a minute. Hold it a second. Have I ever lied to you?" Robby stalled, trying to pin a vague picture in his mind. As Kevin's eyes reddened at the rims, Robby recalled last night's ad—Santa Claus in the local Mannheim Department Store.

"Hey," he shouted, giving Kevin's shoulder a shake. "Hey. Listen, Kev. We're going to see Santa. He's visiting here just one day and I know where. I'm sure he'll be glad to see you," Robby babbled, trying to shape with words Kevin's crumpling features.

As the boy quieted, Robby grabbed his mittened hand and pulled him along. The business district was a good six blocks away, and Robby reflected with annoyance that his mother wouldn't let him ride a bike with Kevin as passenger.

They passed some boys with ice skates hanging around their necks, and Robby made elaborate shrugging gestures toward the ones he knew, without stopping to explain. If he hurried, and Mrs. Boyd got back early, he could get some skating in.

To Robby's dismay, the store was crowded with kids as well as grownups. What if Santa had only special times? He pulled his jacket open, suddenly oppressed by the wet wool steaming the air, then lifted Kevin slightly to speed their pushing through the people. He'd give Kev a quick look and get out.

Glancing around, Robby saw a line of kids, some with mothers, standing along a railing on the mezzanine and hurried Kevin up the short flight of stairs. In an alcove at the line's other end, was the familiar red suit and beard. Raising Kevin to his own eye level, Robby shouted, "See? See him? There he is. Just like I said."

"I want to tell him," Kevin said.

Robby put the boy down. "Tell him what? He's busy."

"I want to tell him."

Observing Kevin's solid stance, Robby knew he could never budge him without his screaming every inch. When he got this way, Robby usually handed him over to his mother. He blew his breath out, disgusted, noting there were at least twenty kids in line. He automatically pulled at Kevin, but the boy crouched back and his eyes began to glisten. "No."

"All right. All right. But you have to get in line. Come on. That's the rule."

Kevin shook loose and backed into a place behind another small boy and his mother. "Unzip your coat," Robby whispered harshly. He glanced at the woman who said, "He's a lucky little boy to have a brother looking out for him."

Robby just nodded. Ever since the Boyds moved in over a year ago, people took the two boys for brothers. Kevin was too focused on his mission, Robbie guessed, to make his usual reply, "He's my friend."

Shifting from foot to foot, Robby noticed each child leaving with a small coloring book and crayons. That's how they get them off Santa's lap, he decided. Clever. Bored with just standing, he did a few knee bends, but Kevin, a small block of concentration, didn't budge, except to follow the child in front.

When Robby was about to make a pillow of his jacket to sit on, Santa finally beckoned to them. "Both of you?" The beard seemed to smile, and Robby recoiled. "No. Not me. I'm—no, just him." He gave Kevin a push, but the boy backed away.

"Hello, little fella," Santa boomed.

"Come on. Santa hasn't got all day," Robby said.

The boy drew further back, and Robby, bending over, saw the frightened set to his mouth. He picked Kevin up. "I'll hold you," he whispered. "You just tell Santa." He had to get out of here. Suppose somebody saw him?

"A skirt gun," Kevin blurted.

Robby almost dropped him. Santa just smiled, nodded and said, "If you're a good boy."

"Is that all, Kev?" Robby whispered.

"A skirt gun," Kevin repeated, as if mesmerized.

Santa waved, and a young woman handed Kevin a coloring book and crayons. Robby picked them up as they fell from Kevin's limp hand, grabbed the hand and pulled him along, jerking him up as his feet stumbled on the stairs.

When they stood outside, Robby released his fury. "You mean we waited in that hot line so you could ask for a lousy squirt gun? Are you crazy?"

Kevin looked down, and Robby's fingers trembled with the urge to whack him one. But Kevin would just start screaming. Robby bit back the words, "you dope, there's no Santa Claus anyway." No telling what the kid would do then. "Come on." Robby strode off. When he realized he still held the coloring book, he whirled, waited for the boy to catch up, tucked it under Kevin's thickly padded arm, and took his other hand.

He moved Kevin along as fast as he could, but still had to make a few stops for Kevin to rest. As they neared their building, Robby's curiosity overcame his anger. "Kevin?" he asked softly. "Kevin, I'm not mad anymore. Just tell me. What did you ask for a squirt gun for?"

Clear blue eyes surveyed him, and Robby had to admit they matched his own. "Mommy won't let me have a gun."

"Yeah?" Robby asked bewildered, although he remembered Mrs. Boyd's opinions on guns.

"Santa Claus has guns," Kevin continued. "So I told him. All the kids have guns and they skirt me. Especially Eugene."

Robby slumped against the door jamb. "But Santa might not bring you what your Mommy doesn't want you to have."

Kevin's gaze was too steady, almost a warning. "They don't know I told him."

As they reached the inside door, Mrs. Boyd opened it. "Ah, the wandering men," she said, smiling.

Robby refused her offer of a cookie, mumbled thanks, and without looking at the coins she put in his hand for babysitting, raced upstairs.

"Can I have my allowance now?" he burst out when he reached the kitchen, where his mother was tearing lettuce at the sink. "My allowance. I have to get something quick."

Would she start yakking now? He never knew what to expect. Sometimes she'd understand without a word. Sometimes she blew sky-high. She put the lettuce down, tore off a paper towel, then marched past him to the bedroom. She returned with a folded dollar bill, her face expressionless.

In the department store he fidgeted in front of three kinds of squirt guns, wondering if Kevin had a special kind in mind. He stroked each type and decided on the middle-priced one. A dollar twenty-nine. A good size for Kevin's hand and Robby couldn't afford more anyway, with the Christmas wrapping paper he still had to get. His grandparents gave him a silver dollar every Hanukkah, but you couldn't spend that. His parents used to give him one special present, though his father always sneaked him an extra dollar. He was too old for the little toy or dreidel game every night. Too old to believe in that bar mitzvah stuff too.

By the time he got home, his mother had left for the extra sales job she had taken for the holidays. Propped against his ice skates was a torn piece of a paper bag with a note on it in her round handwriting. "Heat meatloaf in refrigerator; practice piano; in that order. Love." He couldn't wait to tell her that you couldn't heat meatloaf in a refrigerator.

After ice skating, he opened a can of peas to go with his dinner. Then he practiced the Chopin Prelude and the Bach Invention and skipped the exercises, telling himself he better get the gun wrapped first. As he tried to crease the paper around the uneven shape, it tore against the gun's plastic edge. This was stupid. He was going to all this fuss just to pretend like the rest of them. Like pretending Dad would get better. That he wasn't that sick. Robby threw the gun on his bed and crossed to the window, pressing his forehead against the cold pane. Why did people go to so much trouble to lie to kids? Didn't the truth hurt more when it was covered up first?

He drew back from the window and glanced at his clock. Kevin would be in bed. Waiting, probably. Suddenly, Robby scampered up and down his room. Maybe Kev would think the noise was the reindeer on the roof. He picked up the torn package and rooted out some old T.B. stickers to hide the rip.

Mrs. Boyd again answered the door and smiled, stepping back inside. "It's Robby," she called, and Robby glanced from her to see Mr. Boyd rummaging under their tree. Usually he was bent over the dining room table, studying for a thesis, whatever that was.

Les Boyd looked up, revealing an unlit pipe in his mouth. He smiled around the stem and jiggled an ornament in greeting.

Robby had forgotten about Mr. Boyd. If a man didn't like guns, he really didn't like them. He cleared his throat and thrust the package behind him. "I . . . uh . . . have to explain about Kevin."

"Want to join us for a cocoa break?"

"No," Robby said quickly. "No thanks. I . . ." he swallowed again. "Mrs. Boyd, Kevin asked Santa Claus for a squirt gun."

Her smile disappeared, and Robby felt sweat prickle beneath his wool shirt. He spoke louder, over the pounding of his heart. "Kevin figures if only Santa knows about it, and you don't like guns, then, you see?"

He brought one hand from behind his back, palm up, holding the package shaped like a gun. Would they hate him now? Figure he didn't respect their holiday? Was it especially bad to give a gun on Christmas? The way they felt?

He saw them exchange glances, and as Mrs. Boyd turned back to him, he added, "I know he doesn't need it. Except it may be the one thing. His proof. Of Santa. You know? Like when you're little and you tell God, if he'll do this one thing, you'll believe . . ." his voice trailed off. Rabbi Keppler's words at his father's funeral beat at his brain. *We cannot ask why. We can only ask His blessing.*

Mrs. Boyd looked concerned, and Robby's eyes sought Mr. Boyd's. "Well, I guess it's up to you. I mean, if you don't care . . . if Kevin finds out. About Santa, I mean."

"A symbol of violence," Mrs. Boyd was saying. "A tacit acceptance—even in play . . ."

"God does not stop dying—I mean killing," Robby mumbled through stiff lips.

Mr. Boyd nodded. "Yes. Only men can stop that."

Robby felt his back against the door and tried to turn the handle behind him. Mr. Boyd moved closer. "Robby. We appreciate what you're trying to do for Kevin. But he can be taught that Santa Claus doesn't like guns."

Robby stepped sideways so he could maneuver through the partly opened door. An image flashed through his mind: the doctor with his hand on his mother's shoulder. "I guess kids can be taught anything," he said.

He jumped as Mr. Boyd's hand gripped his shoulder. "How's the bar mitzvah practice going?"

"Oh, I'm not planning on it."

"Really?" Mr. Boyd rubbed his forehead with his pipe. "What's the problem?".

"I don't see the point. What good will it do?"

"What good is it supposed to do?"

He sounded like his father, Robby thought. "Oh, make me a man."

"You know better than that. It means you take your place among Jewish men. To stand up and be counted."

"Big count. My grandpa and my aunt will be there."

"We'll be there, Robby. We're looking forward to it."

Robby turned his head to look straight at Kevin's father. "You are? Why?"

"We think it's an important step in your life. We want to be there—as witnesses."

Robby shrugged and began backing out the door when Mr. Boyd added, "And I think it's about time you called me Les, don't you? Tell your mother I said so."

"Sure," he said. Mr. Boyd seemed to be waiting. "Sure, Les," he whispered, mostly to himself.

When he returned home, Robbie glanced away from the sofa where his mother and father used to sit reading, and saw the menorah on the bookcase's top shelf. It stood empty of candles now that Hanukkah was over. Waiting. Like the Christmas ornaments that the Boyds packed and unpacked. On the end table was a picture of his grandfather with his arm around his father's shoulder, his father holding him as a baby. Robby squinted his eyes against the blurry images, imagining how it would've looked with him in it now. He wondered if his grandpa was imagining it, too.

Turning abruptly, Robby studied the clumsy package, the gun protruding from rips in the paper. He withdrew the gun and squeezed the trigger, the veins rising on the back of his hand. The clock ticked loudly, startling him. His mother wouldn't be home for another hour. This should have been her vacation, too, until school started. He glanced at the piano. She was too tired to play lately. He riffled through the exercise book with his free hand, and a slip of paper fell out. It read, "15 minutes equals one chocolate marshmallow ice cream cone."

After laying the gun on the piano back he decided to tell Kevin that Santa left the gun with Robby because Kevin's parents didn't allow guns. They make kids nasty, like Eugene. But if Kevin would point out Eugene, Robby would make sure he never bothered Kevin again.

He frowned. What if Kevin asked why Robby could use the gun? Robby tapped a piano key a few times, then smiled. He'd tell Kevin that older men could do things to protect little kids. And sometimes kids have to do things to protect their parents. When Kevin grew up he'd understand.

Satisfied, he lowered himself onto the piano bench. Chocolate marshmallow was for little kids. He didn't really like it anymore.

Laugh Lines

The last thing Florrie wanted was to get into a fight with her hairdresser and his colorist. It would be like calling your surgeon a twit right before he operated on you. But there she was. Embroiled. And it had all started out with a simple request. Florrie wanted to wear her hair long, gently curled, and delicately streaked with ash-moon. But Wally refused to permanent her hair if she colored it again.

"Look! It's breaking at the part," he shrieked, holding up the back of her hair like a squirrel's tail.

"I have plenty to spare," Florrie said. She had very thick hair, the consistency and resiliency of straightened steel wool. "And Agnes says she's going to give me a different tint anyway."

"I don't care if she's going to give you a fudge sundae."

Florrie blinked. Wally's choice of expletives often distracted her from the main point. But Agnes towered behind him, immaculate in her rubber gloves. "I use nothing harmful," she said, pressing her huge hands on her bony Swedish hips. "You insist on too tight a curl." She stared boldly into the mirror and Wally's widening eyes reflected there.

"Well, actually," Florrie interposed. "I think that's my fault. I don't like to have permanents often."

"Then just let me cut it short," Wally said. "You've been wearing it long for *years*."

"But my husband and I like it this way," Florrie said, wincing at his emphasis. "And I have to have a permanent in order to wear it long. I can't be setting it day and night." She couldn't drag her husband into it again. It sounded too much like "my daddy can beat up your daddy."

"Then go to your natural color," Wally said. "It's probably lighter now anyway from graying."

"It's dark brown," Florrie said.

Agnes sniffed. "She can't go brown. It's too aging. Look at her skin. She needs the light around her face."

"She needs to have her hair off her face. To combat the down lines—there around the mouth and eyes." Wally pointed.

"Color makes the skin look fresh," Agnes insisted. "She's yellow as it is."

"Well, her chin needs a different length cut anyway," Wally said. "The bulge underneath is becoming noticeable, especially when she wears a turtleneck."

Florrie lifted her head in a suddenly recalled exercise from high-school gym: pretend a string is going right through your center and out the top of your head. "Just a minute," she said, her jaw unnaturally tight.

"I haven't got all day to argue." Wally clamped his arms across his chest. "If you want your own way, I don't know why you come to a stylist. Besides, I gave you that look in the first place. I need the freedom to design another one. Or what's the point?"

"I appreciate your problem," Florrie began, having memorized a line from a book on assertiveness. But before she could continue, Agnes whooshed out so deep a sigh that, had she been one of Florrie's children, Florrie would have snapped, "Say it! Don't make a production out of it."

Agnes, however, needed no encouragement. "I really can't be responsible for every whim a woman has at a certain age," she said.

"You chose this color in the first place," Florrie said. "I was only twelve weeks younger then." She saw them exchange a look over her head. Every fiber in her body knew that look. Her parents had used it when she wanted to go steady for the first time. Her husband and his partner had used it when she offered to do their taxes after a night-school accounting course. Her son and daughter wore the look on college vacations whenever she opened her mouth to say more than, "Dinner is ready." The look included a barely perceptible shrug, an understanding too deep for words, an assessment of her mentality that kindness and forbearance alone prevented them from sharing with her.

But she had trusted her hairdresser. Here, where people literally let their hair down, she had put her whole head in their creative hands. She never complained when her ends split or the color faded, or when it took two weeks before the cut looked decent. She needed them to come through for her. And now the people she had trusted were exchanging *the look*. Maybe even labeling her—blackest mark of all—a suburban bitch.

Meanwhile Wally threw up his hands, then let one arm descend on the shoulder of Agnes, his comrade now that they had a common enemy. "Listen," he said. "Our job is to satisfy the customer. To make her as attractive as our skills allow. Why don't we skip the color for a few weeks. And let me just cut off the old ends of the permanent."

"Beyond those old ends my hair is absolutely straight!" Florrie pulled at her hair and bent forward to reveal her part. "And I'm solid brown for a good four inches before you see any gold at all. I need help *now*..." The words trailed into a howling lament. Florrie let her voice rise and dip, beyond caring if she went bald or enraged them. She would not give them the satisfaction of knowing her forty-sixth birthday was coming in two weeks, even though they thought she was having turning-forty fits. All that happened when she had turned forty was she got the flu twice in one month and couldn't keep her appointment with the admissions office at the local college until a week after classes began. So now she was a college graduate who knew that long, lightly streaked hair let her still look sexy, and that she had never had the cheekbones for cap cuts, or shingles, or the boy's look, or poodle cuts, or whatever they renamed them every time she was tricked or flattered into trying them.

She put her hands over her admittedly round face. "Please," she said. She felt a cape being tied around her shoulders.

"I'll trim the ends—then permanent just the new growth," Wally said stiffly. "But first I want a conditioner pack on the hair for thirty minutes."

Florrie looked up, wondering if gratitude shone in her eyes and half-hoping it didn't.

"We can do a temporary tint on the part—where there's new growth," Agnes said coldly. "It will last only through three shampoos, you know."

Florrie didn't know if she should cheerily admit that it meant three good weeks for her. Some people shampooed daily, fluffing out their dandelion haloes self-righteously, as though getting rid of oil were an ecological necessity.

Her friend Lynn walked in during Florrie's conditioning and approached her gingerly. "That you? Florrie?"

"So far," Florrie said.

"I thought your car was in the shop."

"Jerry is picking me up."

"You let him see you like this?"

"He saw me have a baby," Florrie said.

"That was twenty years ago," Lynn said, shaking her head. She left to get shampooed and then sat next to Florrie and began the usual recital of her woes, beginning when Bernie had first called six months ago to say he would not be home for dinner and he was seeing the best divorce lawyer in his firm, so she'd better see one, too. "He drives a DC something and wears a gold chain," Lynn continued.

"Bernie?" Florrie had lost the thread.

"No. Elaine's ex. And his new wife is pregnant."

In silent communion they both contemplated Elaine. Her ex-husband was a neurosurgeon with a new nurse. The story line was as inevitable as wrinkles, but, because she had been the first in their group, they were caught unprepared.

"Wasn't there a song or poem—'Grow old along with me'?" Lynn asked.

"I am, Lynn, I am," Florrie said and was relieved to hear her friend laugh.

"Must go," Lynn said. "His highness is beckoning with yon curling iron."

Florrie wondered if Lynn remembered the rest of Browning's poem, "The best is yet to be, the last of life for which the first was made." Of course, in his day, you were probably dead by fifty.

Wally delegated her permanent to a Priscilla that Florrie didn't remember seeing before. All of Wally's assistants tended to blend into a mass of tight jeans over thirty-two-inch hips and fashionable hairstyles that seemed to switch from head to head, above perfectly unlined, bored faces.

Priscilla dumped a basket of curlers in Florrie's lap, handed her a sheaf of tiny tissues, and said, "Give me a gray and then a white."

Florrie looked up, smiling. "Usually they do all gray in one area, and then all white," she said.

The girl looked back in iron disbelief. Then she fished a card from her pocket. "See? Alternate white and gray."

Florrie didn't say, "It's still alternate the other way." Maybe the others had been wrong. Maybe it made no difference. She held up a tissue that was snatched from her hand. Startled, she held out a gray curler.

"White," the young girl snapped.

Florrie jumped. "I don't want too strong a curl," she ventured.

"That depends entirely on how long the solution is in," the girl said. "Most people think the size of the curler matters. It doesn't. Please keep your head still."

Florrie concentrated—white, gray, white, gray. The girl sounded as if she knew what she was doing, and Florrie didn't want to distract her. She could hear Wally laughing with another customer. Maybe it was a good sign that he wasn't worried.

"I hope they're going to cut off these dead ends," the girl said.

"I had a conditioner," Florrie said.

"The hair is dead."

Lynn passed by, waggling her fingers goodbye, her short cut still shorter. Not a dead hair anywhere, Florrie was sure.

Florrie was just rising from the washbowl when Jerry arrived. He stood in the doorway to the shampoo room as if he were marooned in a strange country and too unsure of the native language to ask directions. Florrie waved, but he blinked several times before raising his eyebrows in recognition.

"I'll meet you in the car," he mouthed, as if talking were forbidden. Then he smiled reassuringly and left.

Wally finally finished squeezing the last strand with his curling iron and waved her off. Immediately she ran to the bathroom mirror to check the results in privacy. A little sob escaped her, but she smiled to perk up the downward lines that Wally lamented. Yes, her hair did curl away from her face in too-tight rolls that would loosen in the same shampoos that promised to drain her color away. But her part did have a few golden glints. Each as costly as the price of gold now. But worth it to beat the dark hole that had sucked away her confidence. She had to face it though: she had maybe four more years of wearing her hair this length. It looked tacky on anyone over fifty, called too much attention to the tendons jutting out of the throat like wires holding her head on straight.

Outside, to her relief, she located the car and slid in next to her husband.

"Lynn's still having post-traumatic stress," she said, as he started the car.

"She never should have left Phil alone last summer."

"She's not her husband's keeper," Florrie said.

When they reached home she joined him in the bathroom, where he was splashing water on his face.

"They say my hair is breaking off," she said.

He peered up through waterlogged eyes. "Looks the same to me."

"Well, it's breaking."

He wiped his face with the small towel she handed him. "I guess we're all falling apart."

"*You?* Where are you falling apart?"

"Look. See those wrinkles? I have thousands all around my eyes. See?" He pressed closer to the mirror. "Lines and lines. Maybe I should use your stuff."

She put her arms around his waist from behind. "Those are laugh lines."

"Really?"

"Truly."

As he turned around, she said, "Would you still love me if I cut my hair?"

"What would make you do a thing like that?"

"To stop it breaking off and falling out."

"Oh."

"So take your choice. Long hair or blond. Who has more fun?"

He examined her. She felt his eyes on her downward lines, her pasty skin, her shadow chin, the incipient jowl. Maybe he and Wally and Agnes could have a joint consultation. With an undertaker. They had cosmeticians. They could make even a corpse look good.

"Well? Seen enough?" she asked.

"I don't know. You've always been blondish."

"Not really."

"But the darker parts are okay. I guess I could go with long for now."

He kept looking.

"Do you want to sleep on it?" she asked.

"I'm just noticing," he said. "You don't have those lines like I do. And you laugh just as much." He sighed.

She now looked closely at the face as familiar to her and as mysterious as her own. Pale, concave indentations, like thumbprints beneath his eyes, brackets around his mouth. When had they deepened from thin, white lines into shadows? And his clear blue eyes, the whites threaded with a few red trails. Was he due for a physical? Her gaze returned to his soft mouth, well-shaped lips, so harshly surrounded by new terrain.

"How do you feel?" she asked.

He looked bewildered. "Fine, I guess."

With a forefinger, she soothed the frown lines between his eyes, then cupped his face in her hands. "Good," she said. Bringing his face close to hers, she kissed the deep corners of his mouth, partly as she had kissed the children's hurts, partly as she had bestowed a silent blessing on their triumphs.

If You Need Me

When Dana glanced over at him, Michael was already dressed, stretched out on the bed, half-watching the TV. Catching her eye, he pointed to his watch. She continued patting on the new anti-wrinkle eye gel, then unhurriedly applied mascara. After thirty years of marriage, she knew that for Michael the hourglass was half-empty while for her it was half-full. She also knew they had plenty of time before Al and Betty arrived. When the phone rang, she finished outlining her lips and automatically held out her hand for Michael to pass the receiver. He didn't like to get the phone and said it was always for her anyway. She blotted her lips, then said hello.

"Mom?"

"Jacob?"

"You got another son?"

"One's enough." Ever since her son's voice had deepened in high school, she rarely recognized it, as he well knew.

"I'm almost finished packing for Mexico City," Jacob continued. "Is it okay if I stop by and borrow Dad's tennis racket and duffel bag?"

"Sure. Oh—Al and Betty'll be here. We're going out for dinner. Care to join us?"

"No thanks. Still have a few errands."

She paused. "What happened to your racket?"

"It seems it got stolen."

"Seems?"

"Well . . . my car got broken into and they swiped my laundry and my racket. And my duffel. Actually, they just took the underwear, not my good shirts. Wrong size or they didn't like my taste."

"When? Where?" Her voice rose and Michael looked over.

"I got a lousy parking space yesterday, a few blocks away, so I left some stuff in the car overnight. Didn't want to make two trips."

"I see," she lied. "Uh, why Mexico City?"

"Business and tennis. The guy I'm seeing used to play tournaments. When he found out I won the Western Doubles way back, he got all excited. Should I let him win?"

"You're awfully sure of yourself."

"He's in his mid-thirties."

"That old, huh."

"See you soon."

She set the receiver down slowly, then met Michael's eyes. After she told him, he sighed. "Could've been worse."

She nodded, trying not to think of what worse was.

"It's really a decent neighborhood," her husband said, reading her expression. "Lots of charm. Old three-flats, old trees. You know he hates high-rises."

"That must be why he lives on the third floor."

"So did we, a hundred years ago. Give or take."

She went to her closet, pretending to look for something, and pulled out a black cotton tunic. She felt Michael's hand on her shoulder.

"Look. They didn't even want his shirts. So why worry?"

It was just silly enough to pry a laugh out of her.

By the time Jacob arrived, Al and Betty were each sipping a glass of wine and expressing their usual disbelief when she and Michael raved about the convenience of living in the city—walking to movies, restaurants, even the hospital.

"The hospital?" Betty said, her hand to her throat.

"Flu shots," Michael said.

"My area's pretty nice, too," Jacob put in. "Lots of trees."

"The city's for young people anyway," Betty insisted. "Too dangerous at our age—all the purse-snatchings, the muggings."

Glancing at Jacob, who had sat down beside her after bestowing a kiss, Dana said, "It helps when you have a doorman and indoor parking." Jacob gave her a benign smile and speared a piece of cheese.

Apparently sensing a cue, Al announced that he and Betty had invested in a great long-term health-care policy.

Dana caught Michael's eye. They were both more amused than annoyed by Al's deft selling of his insurance products as "investments."

"Isn't it a little premature?" Dana asked. "My parents are still debating it in their eighties."

"You might consider buying it for them," Al said, not missing a beat. "In the long run, you're only protecting yourself, you know. From their catastrophic nursing home costs."

Jacob stood up to leave. "You mean each generation should buy it for the prior generation?"

"I wouldn't worry about that right now," Dana said quickly. "Which reminds me, we have dinner reservations. It's just a short walk."

"Right," Jacob said. "Remember: Life is uncertain; eat dessert first." He waved goodbye with the tennis racket, adding, "And thanks."

"Mexico City?" Betty said, after the door had closed behind him. "They have terrible pollution. I hope Jacob has had his shots."

"I'm sure his company sees to that," Dana said, not at all sure.

At dinner Al asked, "What is it Jacob does again?"

"Management consultant," Michael said.

Dana leaned back, sipping her wine as she watched Michael launch into an explanation. Hard as it was to believe, their freewheeling, free-spending little boy had metamorphosed into a man who advised companies worth millions of dollars.

After dessert, Al and Betty graciously announced that was the best Italian food they'd ever had in the city. They even stopped looking behind them on the walk back to pick up their car and head for the suburbs.

Once again, Dana was seated before the mirror, wiping off her makeup with a new miracle cleanser, then smoothing on the throat-firming cream and the enriched, overnight moisturizer. She used these products with the same resigned obedience she gave her parents' newest theory on nutrition or government programs—it can't hurt and who knows.

Michael was already in bed, watching a movie, when the phone rang. This time Dana recognized her son's voice.

"It was great seeing you and your well-informed friends again."

"Watch what you say, or I'll sic Al on you until you're knee-deep in theft insurance."

"You win. Actually, I called to give you my hotel."

"Good thinking," Dana said, chagrined at not having asked him for it. "I'll get a pen."

He carefully recited and spelled out the name and post office box of the hotel, including the street address and his room number. When she thanked him, he said, "Wait. Let me give you the 800 number of their U.S. office, too."

"Fine," she said, and dutifully wrote it down.

"And you better take the travel agent's home and work number," he said. "She's a workaholic. You can call her any time."

"Okay." She added the phone numbers of the paragon who never slept.

"That's it. See ya in a week or so."

"Did you get your shots?"

"Is that a trick question?"

"It's a mother's question. Mexico City has the worst pollution."

"No shots. But I'll have enough antibiotics with me to start a small pharmacy. Or arouse suspicion. And we'll be playing on an indoor court. Sleep well."

"Sure. Have fun."

Dana smoothed lotion on her arms and said, "That was Jacob. He wanted to tell us where he'd be."

Michael nodded, his eyes on the screen.

Suddenly, she felt a twinge of discomfort. Although Jacob's job had always required some travel, he'd never given such detailed information before. She showed Michael the list, concealing her uneasiness by joking that their son had given her everything but his Social Security number. Did Jacob still need to know his parents could rescue him if things went wrong? The thought hollowed her insides with fear. She and Michael wouldn't be here forever. She wanted Jacob to trust his own judgment. Maybe the car break-in had upset him more than he let on.

After getting into bed, she pulled the covers to her chin and tried to focus on the flickering screen. But she was seeing Jacob, at three, sobbing with terror as he boarded the nursery school bus. Jacob at five, refusing to wear his Halloween mask because it scared him. And Jacob refusing to go into the basement where, he assured them, spiders were hiding. All outgrown. All forgotten. Until now. Was there a frightened child still huddled inside the man who projected competence and self-assurance? Was he still depending on them to light up the dark places? Or was this the return of the older mother syndrome, the over-reaction from having an only child in your late thirties?

When Michael turned off the TV, Dana had difficulty falling asleep. She finally recalled a rule for sleep disorders. Don't stay in bed staring at the ceiling. Get up. She got up, padded into the kitchen and stared into the refrigerator. Pathetic. A tofu something. Old spaghetti sauce. Browning lettuce. Hearing a sound, she turned. Michael was blinking at her, his hair standing up in tufts and she felt an odd pang. At that moment he seemed to be as vulnerable as his son. Though still a handsome man, the gray hair that had begun as a streak in his twenties, had turned completely white, and he looked old. She probably looked like that to him, except her ever-multiplying gray strands were buried in gold highlights. Fooling nobody. Certainly not old friends who warned them it was time to worry about nursing homes and muggings.

Turning back to the refrigerator, she pulled out the fruit drawer. Two apples rolled forward.

"What're you doing?" Michael asked.

She picked up an apple. It looked shriveled, like those wizened apple-faces she'd seen at an art show. Once the juice was gone, everything caved in, moisturizer or no moisturizer.

She sighed. "Why did Jacob need to make sure we could find him?"

"You don't want to eat that, honey," Michael said.

She tossed the ancient apple into the garbage. "But what is he afraid of?" Before Michael could answer, her words reverberated in the refrigerator with new meaning. She slammed the door shut. "My God, Michael . . . you know what he was doing?"

Her husband reached his hand up to smooth the tufts. "What you said. Making sure we know how to reach him."

Her voice climbed the scale. "But not for *his* sake."

Michael raised his eyebrows in a silent "so?"

"He was trying to make sure we could reach him—if *we* needed *him.*" She shook her head, torn between dismay and relief. "He thinks—he thinks we're . . . old."

They stared at each other as if they were looking into distorted mirrors. Then her husband gave a small, unsuccessful laugh. "I didn't think we looked that bad tonight. We certainly didn't sound old—like Al and Betty, conjuring up the dangers of city living."

"That's it!" Dana said. "They scared him."

"Jacob? He thinks he's living in paradise."

"Not about himself. About us. *Our* safety. *Our* stress." *Our* mortality, she added, silently. Sometimes, when she smoothed the moisturizer over her face she couldn't help but feel the chin and cheek bones—and imagine the skull with its empty eye sockets. The end result of all her preservatives. But, she reminded herself, a very *very* long way off.

Michael cleared his throat, obviously looking for a consoling word. "No big deal. He's an adult. He's figured out we won't be here forever."

They fell silent. Michael's parents had died over a decade ago. Her parents were playing golf in Palm Springs. Sure, they were slowing up a bit. But Mom had bounced right back after her gallbladder operation. The only time she complained of pain was when Dana visited. She said Dana made her laugh and it hurt her stitches. "Somehow it never occurred to me that Mom and Dad wouldn't be here. I've even been planning how to celebrate their anniversary next year. As if there wasn't any doubt that . . ."

"Stop it," Michael said. "They're fine. And happy. Just like us."

"It still wouldn't hurt to call . . . check on them."

"At this hour? You'll scare them to death."

She had to laugh. "Okay. I just don't want Jacob to—to worry about us."

"Maybe it's a new phase he's going through. He'll outgrow it."

Dana tilted her head. "Does that mean we can stop worrying about *him*?"

Tilting his head in imitation, Michael said, "You—a mother—are asking me that?"

She nodded a touché. "I remember asking Mom once, while Jacob was going overboard being a teenager, 'When does it stop—the worrying?' And she said, 'I'll let you know.'"

Michael grinned. "Remember the day after he got his driver's license? He got a ticket for making a U-turn in front of a policeman's car and we paid the fine. I say let the kid worry. Serves him right—thinking we're old."

"I say let's bill him for one of those long-term care policies."

They smiled at each other, Michael eyeing her speculatively, a look she recognized.

"Let's go to bed," he said. "I've thought of another way to relieve stress."

Following him back to the bedroom, Dana pretended to fluff her hair. "I bet you have. You city men just love to flirt with danger."

The Nature of the Game

Beth suggests they play poker—to pass the time. She and her son, Zach, are in the hospital waiting room. His wife is having a caesarean. The doctors insisted this was necessary, Zach had assured her on the phone. But no need to worry. They're sure everything will be fine.

She came right over. He hadn't asked her to, and she was afraid to ask permission. He is capable of saying no, a hard-won ability engendered in a therapist's office after many years, a cost in time and money that he lays at her door. She accepts it.

"You mean you brought a deck of cards along?" He's incredulous, amused, a little disdainful. "I guess conversation is risky, huh?"

Although Beth accepts responsibility for the past, she has stopped apologizing. The fruit of her own later years in therapy—an adventure inspired by his successful outcome. Which she's told him. She suspects, however, that hers hasn't been as productive. An ongoing problem with confrontation. Which he's told her.

"You can play solitaire, if you'd rather." A dare? Or a bluff.

He raises that one eyebrow, a comment she's never fully deciphered. Skepticism? Wariness? Calculation? She's caught herself doing it, but can't latch on to the reason. He pulls a chair to the other side of the coffee table in front of the small sofa she's sitting on. He leans forward. "Deal."

She shuffles. He cuts. She flicks the cards, quickly, economically. He could've suggested gin rummy. She could've, too. She's glad she didn't. Poker feels right. They've never played it together.

"Jan's mother is flying in. She'll be here by tonight."

155

She nods. He told her that already. Does he mean that then she should leave? Gabe wants to come by after work. She studies her cards. Two queens, ace of clubs, two fives. She hates throwing away an ace, but two pair isn't bad. Ambivalence is second nature to her.

He passes over two cards, face down.

She slides two cards from the top of the deck. He takes them, positions them in his hand. Was he born with a poker face? No. He was terrified of water. Bathtub, Lake Michigan. Sat on a blanket at the beach, his back to the water, and whimpered, his round face scrunched up with indignant fear. A beautiful boy—no, gorgeous. Long blue eyes like his father's. Blond hair, like hers, falling in old-fashioned ringlets. When he was almost four, her father insisted she take him to a barber. People will start treating him like a girl, he'd said. Beth doubted it, but doubted herself more. At the barber's, she expected the cliché tears of sitcoms. But ever the master of the unanticipated reaction, he watched, fascinated, even wanted to use the clipper himself.

"Tough decision?" Zach's dry tone.

She slips the ace beneath the deck. "One. I'm taking one."

Eyebrow. "What're we playing for?" A pause of impeccable timing. "I mean, pennies? Pearls? Pens?" They each have an unplanned collection of pens. They buy some on impulse, receive others as gifts. She and Gabe gave Zach a Mont Blanc about ten years ago. He can afford to buy his own now.

"Let me think," she says, focusing on the card she drew. Incredible. A third five. With the queens, a full house. A sure winner. Most he can have is three of a kind. "Pens," she says. "I mean pennies."

"Don't tell me you brought your jar." Perfect deadpan. He always breaks her up. Knows her jar is the family doorstop, paperweight, handy when something heavy is needed. But never a source of pennies. Once in, never out.

"No. But we can call all coins pennies." She indicates his rolled up shirtsleeve. "Cufflinks and buttons, too."

He nods, impressed. He likes quick thinking—quick solutions. Yet he doesn't attribute his success as a consultant to that. It's handling people, he's informed them. Pointedly. He lays that at her knee, too. A PhD in learning to handle his mother. A mother who could yell one minute, be sensitive and understanding the next. Inconsistent. Untrustworthy. A replica, as it came out in therapy, of her stepfather. Nurture sometimes overtakes nature.

"Okay." He reaches into his pants pocket, pulls out some coins, places two pennies on the table. "I bet two."

She empties her coin purse into the plastic ashtray, fishes out four pennies. "I see your two, and raise you two."

"Picked a good one, right?"

She fights a smile. A big bluffer. "See me or fade."

A chuckle. "Where'd you learn that?"

"TV. James Garner in 'Maverick'."

He shakes his head. "Okay. I'll see you. Or die of curiosity."

She spreads her hand. "Full house."

He shows his. Two kings and a matching ace, probably his original holding, and a couple of small ones. "I'd say overkill." He pushes his pennies toward her. "You should've picked pearls."

"Of wisdom?" Ouch. That was a mistake.

He eyes her. "Don't get in over your head." Picks up the deck. "My deal."

He shuffles the cards, then gracefully spins out five each. He has long fingers, stretches well over an octave when he plays the piano. Quick flash of a seven-year-old muttering bitterly as he's forced to practice. Suddenly interrupts his harangue to announce, with awe, "That's a beautiful chord."

"You missed your chance to say 'read 'em and weep'," he says, studying his hand.

"That takes four aces or a royal flush, doesn't it?"

"Nope. It's whenever you win."

"I'll remember next time."

Eyebrow. "You counting on there being a next time?"

"Have to," she says, equally deadpan.

As if triggered by her words, he looks up. "I better check with the nurse. See what's happening."

She stands, but he waves her down. "I'll be right back. Watch the pennies." He smiles.

It doesn't mean she's forgiven. He smiles at everyone. Almost everyone. He's more frugal with words. The ones she wants to hear. But she's afraid time is running out. Marriage uses up a lot of time. So does fatherhood. And friends. His sister, too. He and Sari are close, thank God. He probably called her first. She'd be here if she were in town. Beth and Gabe are somewhere on the list. But she doesn't know how far down. She recoils at the thought. Smacks of high school.

He returns, frowning. "You can never get a straight answer."

"Is anything wrong?"

"I don't think so. But I don't know how long it's supposed to take."

Neither does she. But she's uneasy. Isn't a caesarean pretty routine by now? She says aloud, "Well, it takes as long as it takes."

He nods, clearly not comforted. She knows he hates, as she does, the automatic *I'm sure everything's fine.* Yet maybe he wants to hear it this time. He taps the waiting cards, sits down, picks them up.

She glances back at hers. They're blurred. She hopes he can't see the wetness in her eyes. Fear can be contagious. A nothing hand. Seven, a six, two fours, a three. Chance at a straight. Does she save the pair, or try for a five. She remembers hearing about filling an inside straight. A stupid bet. Who cares anyway? Jan is a sweetheart. A schoolteacher who started a chess club for first-graders. They love it. Beth once told Gabe that Jan was too smart to teach school, but she's ashamed for thinking that. Kids deserve the best.

"Well?" He's drumming on the table. Well-cared for nails. She remembers one of those thumbnails bitten so deeply they put Band-Aids on it and promised him a portable radio if he'd stop. Eventually, he did. For his piano teacher.

She breaks the pair, slides over a four. "One."

He pushes a card toward her, then peels off three. He's keeping a pair. They're opposites. She suppresses a pang.

"Want to look at your card?"

She grabs it up. A five! She filled the straight. What's going on? Lucky at cards, unlucky at love?

"That bad?" he asks.

She blanks her face. "I bet two pennies."

"That good."

He files his new cards. "Two pennies and I raise you two pennies." He shoves a nickel towards her pile, takes out five pennies, leaves four.

She feels a hollowness in her belly. She lost two babies before Zach and his sister. Not by caesarean. Just born too soon. Jan is almost forty. Everything is timing. She pushes four pennies toward him, adds the nickel.

"Is that a nickel or a penny extra?" He sounds annoyed.

"It's a real nickel. I'm raising you five pennies."

"So that's the way it's gonna be," he says.

"You started it."

"Did I?" The eyebrow flicks. She files it away. Chicken or the egg.

He spins a dime onto the table. "Nine to see you—" he throws in a quarter. "And raise you twenty-five big ones."

"You can't do that." Automatic. Her "fairness" monitor has kicked in. The same stupid reaction she had when he was five or six. Checkers. Rummy. She played to win, leaving him frustrated, in tears. Her father would lose on purpose, but Zach never caught on.

"Why not? Too rich for your blood?"

"There's got to be a limit. Like when Gabe played nickel-dime. I remember him saying you can't raise more than a certain amount." Damn. She's still quoting authority. It never worked with her father. He'd dismiss it with, "you believe everything you hear or read, kiddo?" Experience was *his* source. One Beth could never equal.

"We didn't set one at the beginning."

"I didn't think of it then." Is she nuts? For a quarter?

"So. Let's make twenty-five cents the limit. Since we didn't say before. Is that fair? Or too steep?"

He reads her like a headline. Always has. She looks at her coins. A couple of dimes. "I don't have a quarter."

"I'll accept your dimes and—" he pauses, head to one side, as if calculating. "Those earrings should be worth—say a buck?"

She waits to make it look like she's thinking. Then nods. Unhooks an earring. Slides it over. "And raise you twenty-five cents."

The eyebrow. "You're playing hardball now. But then, you always do."

It stops her breath. He's right. She's still trying to win. But now she's stuck. Can't lose.

He throws a dollar bill on the table. "I see you and raise you the limit."

She's totally lost count now, so she parrots him.

He smiles as if he knows she has no idea what she's betting. Points to the other earring.

She dislodges it, tosses it out.

"Okay. I see you. Watcha got, ma'am."

She slowly releases one card at a time.

He whistles. "Straight beats a full house, right?"

She nods, miserable.

"You're supposed to say 'read 'em and weep.'"

She can't blink the tears back now. *Please don't ask me,* she begs. *Don't ask me why.*

"Okay." His voice softens. "I've got four of a kind. So it's my turn to say it." He begins, "Read 'em and—"

The nurse is coming towards them. They both stand. Beth leans on the sofa back to steady herself. Then she sees the woman is smiling. "How is she," they ask, almost simultaneously.

"Mother is fine—not awake yet. But you can see the baby. Through the nursery window."

"Baby?" he says. As if he's not sure why she's mentioning a baby.

"A beautiful baby boy." Proudly. The messenger willing to take full credit.

He repeats it, tasting the words. "A beautiful baby boy."

Beth starts to sob. Feels his arms around her. Hears him whisper, "It's okay." She finally takes a shaky breath, looks up to see tears in his eyes. "It's okay," he says again.

It's been years since he's said, "I love you." But you play the hand you're dealt.

They follow the nurse down a long hall to a large window. The room behind is filled with little bassinets on wheels. A few men and women are waving at wriggling babies with faces red from crying, fists tight, as if holding on to their own fingers offers some safety. The illusion someone is there.

Disappearing inside, the nurse reappears holding a tiny body in a blanket. She brings it closer to the window. Sleepy lids open to a slit. Beth thinks she sees a flash of blue before the lids squeeze shut. She's heard most babies start with blue eyes. The wispy hair has a reddish tinge. Zach is staring at the baby. Half-murmuring to himself. "A little boy . . ." He touches her arm. "Is he really so beautiful?"

Surprised, she pretends to study the little red face, its lips pursed, searching for a nipple. The nurse has unwrapped him to show his tiny arms and legs pumping. Beth nods. "Yes. For a baby, he's beautiful."

He laughs. "I can always count on you for the truth, right?" Before she can take that in, he adds, "I'm a father."

"Sure are," she says.

"Wish Grandma and Grandpa could've seen him."

An inner lurch. He was so close to her father. As an adored grandchild, Zach could do what she never could—laugh at his grandfather's tricky tactics in an argument. Tease him about his attempts to manipulate. Jolly him out of an automatic criticism. Their relationship brought out the best in both. She could only stand and watch. Grateful but outside the charmed circle. She becomes aware that Zach is still speaking. The last words reach her like an echo. "I never would've survived if he'd been *my* father."

She can only stare at him. He's not smiling. But there's a tenderness softening his eyes and lips.

"Thanks for the game," he says. "It helped." Now the lines around his mouth disappear in a smile. "You owe me a bundle."

"I know. I'll sign a note." She'd sign over everything she owns. But he doesn't want it.

"I'm going to see Jan. If she's awake they'll bring the baby to her." Beth's signal to go. She'll call Gabe at work. Tell him the good news. Zach touches her shoulder. "Wait. Don't leave." She glances up, confused. "Have to give you a chance to get even." Poker pause. "It's the least I can do, Grandma."

He walks away, tall, composed, more beautiful than ever. Her son. Her face is wet as she walks back to the waiting room. She'll never know for sure what he's thinking. But then, that's the nature of the game.

Stockpiling

The shopping bag Lily had brought from home dug into her arm. She hadn't planned to lug it around a department store, but Sam wouldn't let her come to the hospital until after lunch, and she couldn't bear waiting at home. They were giving him more tests this morning. But they always hedged the answers. She often wanted to ask the doctors if they had a personal preference: giving patients an ounce of hope before plunging them into despair; or letting them sink slowly into despair, until they were certain of success.

Glancing around for any distraction, she noticed a pair of dark red leather gloves on a counter. Although she'd already bought a sweater the exact cobalt blue of Jody's eyes for her birthday next month, she couldn't resist. Two gifts wouldn't be overdoing it, especially for a twelve-inch, three-pound preemie who had blossomed into a thirty-year-old, five-foot-two-and-a-half-inch woman who insisted on that half inch. While the saleswoman wrote up the sale, Lily checked her watch. Everything was relative—thirty years melted in a second, while an hour waiting for news from the hospital snowballed into an eternity. Another hour to kill. What an awful expression. Time was all anyone had—and never enough of it. She placed the gift in her shopping bag and headed for the escalator.

It was Donna who had taught Lily to be alert for the unexpected heart-stopper. Exotic brass napkin rings to enliven old tablecloths. An antique ice bucket to hold cookies. Donna called it "earned serendipity." Amused at what she deemed a high-end rationalization, Lily responded, "How about creative solutions to unperceived needs."

"You mean like getting married?" Donna said, deadpan.

They'd burst out laughing, delighted with themselves. Eventually, shopping together became an exciting tutorial for Lily. Certainly different from the childhood expeditions with her mother—poring over dress patterns. In those days, serendipity was finding the perfect fabric and buttons on sale the same day. For grown-up Lily, after marriage and moving to suburbia, serendipity was meeting Donna at the orientation for their children's play school. Discovering that they used the same hair colorist, and that Donna's son and Lily's daughter would be attending the same grammar school the following year, Donna said it proved they were fated to meet.

One day, after they'd begun seeing each other regularly, Donna said, "Lily, with your figure you should be wearing things that show it off. We're going shopping. Change your style."

Lily admitted, a bit shyly, that Sam's aunt often sent "care packages" of expensive, only slightly worn clothes. "There's old as in antique lace and there's old as in leftovers," Donna said. But first they had to clean out Lily's closet to make way for the new. While Lily gratefully accepted Donna's labeling the discards as, "way beyond the sell-by date," she tried to hang on to a fuzzy yellow jumper. They were laughing and pulling it between them when Sam, returning early from work, announced that he'd always hated it.

"You never told me that," Lily said.

"I said jumpers were for kids in school."

"Oh," Lily said and let a grinning Donna stuff it into a plastic bag.

It was their first day of shopping together—and Donna's subtle acknowledgment of Lily's price range, considerably below her own—that cemented their friendship.

Pausing now at a cosmetics counter, Lily remembered the afternoon they spent on Oak Street, being "made over" at the famous Marilyn Miglin's. "I don't think twice the money means twice as beautiful," Lily had whispered when they examined the results.

"I can use all the help I can get—or buy," Donna said.

"Come on," Lily said, "You've got to know you're beautiful when you look in the mirror."

Without hesitation Donna said simply, "but as soon as I look away, I forget."

Saddened by the insecurity, and moved by the trust that Donna's remark implied, Lily couldn't speak. Donna, however, patted Lily's cheek and smiled. "It's all illusion anyway, sweetie. Like placebos."

Now, after another glance at her watch, Lily sighed, then shifted the bag to her other arm and rode the escalator up. Designer dresses. She averted her eyes and continued up another floor. Less than ten years after they met, while Donna fought Hodgkins Disease, Lily had combed the stores, bringing home armfuls of dresses for her friend to choose from, both of them reassuring each other that she'd be wearing them the coming season. Through the wakeful nights following Donna's death, Lily would summon up her friend's wan delight, replaying their conversations about books, accessories, and children as if memory were merely another form of reality. After all, if Donna had moved to another city, that wouldn't mean she didn't still exist. It wasn't like Lily's father who had died before Lily was two. She'd once confided to Donna that without any memories of "Daddy Joe" it was as if he'd never existed.

"Hey," Donna said. "Mine left when I was a kid. Mom got me a nanny and probably never even missed a card game at the club. *I* knew *he* existed. He just didn't care that *I* did."

It was then that Lily told Donna about her two miscarriages. Lily finished matter-of-factly, "So they kept me in bed with Jody. She was still four weeks early."

"And you named her after 'Daddy Joe,'" Donna whispered, not a question.

Lily nodded. She hadn't even admitted it to her mother. "So he existed," Donna said, and Lily felt a swelling of relief that she had a friend who understood.

The escalator ended in Housewares. Once Jody graduated college, they'd moved into the small condo downtown and no longer needed the "heart-stoppers" that Donna had treasured. But after Lily stopped working, she began walking home after her exercise class or lunch with a friend. Along the way, she'd stop in the stores lining Michigan Avenue, and during sales, began to stock up on photo albums and silver trays for eventual weddings and anniversaries, stuffed animals for the inevitable babies, and scarves and wallets for Christmas and Hanukkah. Sam joked about her "stockpiling," as he called it, saying it was a good thing they could afford to save all that money. But she'd quoted Donna: "It never hurts to be prepared."

She paused at a display of embroidered tablecloths, reminded of the sampler she'd made when she was five and her mother had taught her to cross-stitch. While helping Lily redecorate, Donna had noticed it among the odds and ends going into storage. Calling it an antique, she had insisted it be framed.

"Thanks," Lily had said drily. "From a child to an antique in one day." Now, whenever she looked at those tiny squares of red, green, yellow, blue and pink, she saw a little girl hunched over an embroidery hoop, proudly calling her mother's attention to her clever use of a different color for each letter and flower.

The truth was, as Lily should have learned after Donna's death, you couldn't always be prepared. No mammograms had found the cancer in her mother's esophagus. No vitamins had prevented it. Lily had already bought a pink flowered bed-jacket for her mother's 70th birthday. She gave it, still in its fancy wrapped box, to the funeral attendant to bury her mother in. Donna had been gone ten years by then, but Lily felt as if a wound had been ripped open. Was grief always fresh?

Unable to sleep after her mother died, and with Jody away at college, Lily began taking sleeping pills. She kept refilling the prescription, explaining to the doctor that she and Sam traveled with tour groups whose days began at sunrise, so she needed to fall asleep quickly. So far, she'd saved almost a hundred pills. A creative solution to the unbearable suspense of living, she thought. A guarantee that she had a choice.

Glancing at her watch, she decided that she could finally leave the store and the memories it had evoked. But when the down escalator moved past the jewelry counter, she again had to avert her eyes. Before she died Donna had given Lily an antique jet pin. "I know you're not into jewelry," she said. But everyone needs one important piece. If only to leave to someone she loves."

Once outside, Lily hurried past Elizabeth Arden's red door. As always, she was reminded of the blouse that she and Donna had dug out of a sales pile during their last post-holiday shopping spree. More suitable for Donna, the black-and-gold paisley brocade was shot through with gold thread and fastened with rhinestone buttons set in thin rims of gold. And marked down to one quarter of its extravagant price. Donna had brushed away Lily's objections, insisting it was the kind of piece that made a statement.

When Jody, ten at the time, decided it would be a perfect pirate costume for Halloween, Lily had not even worn it yet. Instead she dug out a black velvet cape her mother had made for her years ago, and sent Jody off as a vampire. Lily wore the blouse to Donna's next party, and told the story, so they both referred to it ever after as "The Pirate Blouse." She also wore it to Donna's memorial service.

There'd been no funeral. Al had chosen to have Donna cremated. No chance to see her in one of the new summer dresses she'd never worn. The gold, heart-stopping blouse was wildly inappropriate, but it was the first time Lily had understood what Donna meant by making a statement. She knew that Donna would have approved.

Lily tiptoed into Sam's room. He lay still, eyes closed, until she rattled the shopping bag. "Hey," he said, then opened his eyes. "Guess what. Jody's flying in tonight. Her case finished up ahead of time. She tried to call, but you'd already left the house."

"Great," Lily managed, trying to seem more surprised than uneasy. She didn't ask why, but obviously Sam must've called his daughter. Jody could rarely leave so quickly. What had he told her? What had the doctors told him? Instead of voicing her questions, she pulled out the cashmere robe she'd been saving for his birthday in September.

Sam grinned. "See? I told her you were probably out shopping."

"Why don't we put it on . . . ?"

"Because 'we' aren't cold. Now *me*, on the other hand . . ."

It hung on his bony shoulders. "I think it'll fit you," he said.

"I was hoping you'd say that. *I* have always wanted a really nice robe, but . . ." she paused for effect, "no one ever thought to give *me* one."

He chuckled.

Who else would find her funny? And vice-versa.

His smile faded. "You're not losing sleep over this, are you?"

"Sleep? That's for wimps."

"Why don't you take Jody shopping when she gets here? Have some fun."

"Jody hates to shop. She uses one of those personal shoppers."

"So you be her personal shopper—if it isn't too personal. You know—if all Jody does is work, she and that husband of hers should've taken jobs here. At least we would've been able to visit them in the courtroom."

"Or sue somebody."

They both had been bereft when Jody had joined her fiancé's law firm. After getting through the years until she'd come home for good after law school, it had never occurred to them that an only daughter could move away.

"She never struck me as the lawyer type—used to dress like a gypsy." He laughed. "Remember that skirt your mother made for her?"

Lily nodded. A riot of different fabrics from all the remnants her mother had collected over the years. "Jody practically slept in it. Even asked me why I didn't sew things like that."

"Why didn't you tell her you were a marketing genius? Helping me build a business?"

"Why didn't you?"

He waved a dismissive hand. "Probably why she became a lawyer. You were a role model. Anyway, didn't you make her a tennis dress? When we won that doubles match?"

Lily nodded again. The year Donna died. The year Donna's son was called out of class to be sent home. The year Jody was a senior. That was the year Lily had felt an urge to do something with her hands and bought a pattern. Then she called her mother, who told her not to read all the directions at once. "And don't look too far ahead."

"Came out pretty good as I remember," Sam continued.

"Yeah, but it took forever. A lot of ripping out seams." She smoothed the heavy cotton blanket. At the time, Sam had remarked that, figuring her hourly income, the dress had cost more than Jody's three years of tennis lessons.

Lily had to ask. Squeezing her fingers together to keep them from trembling, she said, "Sam. Did you call her? Jody?"

He raised his eyebrows, clearly surprised. "No. She said she wanted to see us."

"Us?"

Frowning, he said, "Yeah. Us. As in you and me. Why?" Then his brow cleared.

"Oh. Sorry. No news. Tests inconclusive. Like those *New Yorker* stories you like."

"So what's next?" she asked. Then, responding to his wry smile, "Oh. More tests."

"Bingo."

When he fell back to sleep, Lily untwisted her fingers. After her mother had finally remarried, she and George, a lifelong bachelor and an only child, were given only a few years to enjoy together. A Pollyanna to the end, her mother declared, despite her second descent into widowhood, that it was worth it. "At least he didn't have to die alone."

Who would want to be the survivor? Lily wondered. The last one left standing. She jerked her head, as if to dislodge the thought, and her glance fell, with relief, on the shopping bag. The gloves would fit the image Jody projected so well. Smart, capable, sophisticated. Lily had once flown to Boston to watch her daughter argue a case while wearing bright red pumps with a crisp navy suit. Like the red lining of the vampire cape, Lily had thought, smiling. Just another costume.

Sam turned and his hand slipped over the side of the bed. Lily took it in hers and rubbed it lightly. His beautiful long fingers, folded casually over the back of a chair, had first attracted her. She looked at her hands, small wrinkled palms like her mother's. Like a monkey's, Sam had once teased her.

Years before, while teaching Lily to hem with tiny stitches, her mother had said, "You can sew anything by hand. It takes longer, but it's much nicer." The thing about hands, Lily thought, was they needed to touch. Like the mouth's need to taste, they were the body's antennae—the front line of knowing. She brought Sam's hand to her lips, and when she looked up, he was smiling at her. "Got no complaints, kid."

She bowed her head to hide her eyes. And what would he make of her pathetic little stockpile of sleeping pills? Once, pointing to her carefully labeled boxes in the closet, he'd said, "You'll run out of people before you run out of stuff to give them." She hurriedly looked toward the ceiling, a trick Donna had taught her to keep mascara from running.

"I was just thinking," she said. "Why wait 'til Jody's birthday. As long as she'll be here, we can celebrate in person."

"Naturally you bought her a present months ago."

"Well, I bought her one present months ago. And another one today. It's serendipity."

"Seren-what?"

"A solution to an unperceived need." At his questioning look, she added, "You know. Like marriage."

"I have a feeling I've been insulted."

"Not really. You solve the problem ahead of time. Before you know what you'll need."

His eyes lit up. "Ah," he said. "Like stockpiling."

Until you run out of people. Or time. Or pills. No! The word cut into her thoughts so forcefully she almost looked to see if someone had spoken. How could she do that to her child? The sole survivor? Her thoughts swerved. The phone call. Very bad news or very good news had to be given in person. No. Don't look too far ahead, Mom had said.

"You better get home—before Jody gets there. I'm not sure she'll have anything to eat on the plane. The one thing you never stockpiled is food. How come?"

"Because I never know what you'll want to eat."

"Go."

"I'm leaving the robe. Wear it. It's warm."

She stopped in a little bakery on her way home. Jody loved tea cookies. They also had fresh bread. She could pick up sliced roast turkey at the deli near her building. It seemed like a feast to her, and she realized she hadn't thought about food since Sam had gone into the hospital—three-and-a-half weeks ago.

After she put the groceries away, she got a big box out of the basement storage room to put the gifts in. They always used to do that when Josie was little, to disguise the contents. Relieved to have completed her preparations, she changed into a pair of soft knit pants and a tunic top, then lay down on the sofa to rest until Jody arrived.

But someone was shaking her shoulder, and she jerked herself upright, calling out, "Sam? Sam?"

"It's me, Mom." Lily's eyes focused on her daughter as if seeing an apparition, and she held her arms out. "Oh, sweetie," she said. "You're here. Was I asleep?"

"Dead to the world," Jody said, hugging her. "My plane got in late, what else is new, and I grabbed a cab."

"Are you hungry? I have fresh bread and your tea cookies."

"My favorite kind of sandwich."

They hugged again, and Lily said quickly, "There's nothing new to add about your father's condition." Nevertheless, she repeated the bald medical facts that Jody had learned from her morning phone call: the MRI had shown a tiny something in the pancreas that had to be watched; and a few more alphabetical tests ahead. Nothing conclusive so far. Lily finished with, "Remember what Grandma always said."

"Don't look too far ahead," Jody finished.

Now it was Jody's turn to explain whatever was on her mind that brought her home, but Lily knew better than to jump in with questions. First they settled themselves in the kitchen with paper plates, coffee, herbal tea, and the fixings. Then came comments about the flight, Jody's recent case, and the pros and cons of living in the city.

"So . . ." Lily waited, moving the cookies around on her plate.

"Why am I here?"

"A good place to start."

Jody took a deep breath. "Naturally, we've been—concerned. And when these next few days opened up, it was obvious. Come see for myself. Not just Dad. But you, too. How are you? Really."

"I shop."

"That bad."

"Not really. I sort of meditate in stores. I remember your father was in a department store with me one time, apparently watching me do my thing. When we finished he asked me if I was praying over every blouse and belt. I must have been engrossed in comparing prices, styles, fabrics, what event or birthday was coming up . . . It certainly takes your mind off everything else."

Jody shook her head, smiling. "Dad's much more observant than people think."

"Absolutely. Though his interpretations need work."

"Remember when we played mixed doubles at that tennis club? What was I? Sixteen?"

Lily nodded. "He told me you were terrified."

"There were all these husband and wife teams—and they were good."

"Sam said that in that first match, the guy told his partner to hit the ball at the kid."

"Yeah."

"Little did he know how hard the kid could hit."

"Little did *I* know. But when somebody hits the ball straight at you, all you really have to do is get your racket on it."

"You did a bit more than that, as I recall."

"I guess. Anyway, I was still terrified until we switched sides and Dad said, 'Honey, we're really beating them bad; how about letting them win a few games?' Can you imagine?"

Lily beamed. "Your father didn't have the killer instinct, but he sure knew what his daughter needed."

As they sat in silence for a minute or so, Lily felt that something was different—and it made her smile to realize that she'd forgotten how it felt to be relaxed. To just let things flow.

"I was wondering . . ." Jody began.

"Wondering what?"

"Where that little embroidery picture is. The one you did when you were little. Grandma told me how proud you were of using up all the colors in her sewing box. I always loved that story."

"It's around here somewhere," Lily said.

"I memorized what it said."

"Really? What did it say?"

Jody pretended to orate. "Seek Home For Rest, For Home Is Best."

"My goodness," was all Lily could manage. She had the sense of being on the verge of an understanding. But no idea of what.

"Didn't Donna get you to frame it?"

Lily nodded.

"She also picked out those cool bead curtains for my bedroom, didn't she? They were turquoise, royal blue and white."

Again, Lily nodded. When Jody didn't continue, she said, "I'm amazed at all you remember. I suppose I thought . . . you weren't paying attention."

Jody's look was direct and, Lily thought, purposeful. "I remember everything, Mom. I even remember that beautiful gold blouse you wouldn't let me wear for Halloween."

Startled, Lily laughed. "The pirate blouse? Are you still upset about it?"

"Not really. Just . . ." Again Lily waited. "Do you still have it?"

"Actually . . . yes."

"Do you wear it?"

"Uh, no."

"You wore it to Donna's . . . memorial, didn't you."

Lily blinked her surprise. "I had no idea . . . you knew that."

"I'd like to have it, if it's all right with you."

Picking at the crust on the bread, Lily said, "Really? Why?"

Jody glanced away, then looked back. "I'm making a quilt. A small one—the kind you hang on a wall. I want to include pieces of fabric that . . . mean something to me. Like that funky skirt Grandma made me. And the red sweater Dad wore playing doubles with me. And I was wondering . . . if you had some stuff . . . you weren't using anymore."

Her mind whirling, Lily felt as if an old wound was being soothed by her daughter's words. How thrilled her mother and Donna would've been! They would've torn apart perfectly good clothes, even their fine furniture coverings, to give this child any scrap she asked for. They would've understood what Lily was only beginning to understand. Why Donna had said, when giving her the beautiful jet pin . . . an important piece to leave to someone you love.

Jody put her hand on her mother's arm. "I didn't mean to make you sad."

"I'm not sad. I'm . . . grateful." To keep her tears back, Lily added, "I've been trying to think of what to get you for your birthday. It never occurred to me that old clothes would be just the thing."